THE
GUARDIAN
HERD

STORMBOUND

Also by Jennifer Lynn Alvarez
The Guardian Herd: Starfire

THE GUARDIAN HERD

STORMBOUND

BY

JENNIFER LYNN ALVAREZ

HARPER

An Imprint of HarperCollinsPublishers

Library of Congress Cataloging-in-Publication Data
Alvarez, Jennifer Lynn, author.
  Stormbound / by Jennifer Lynn Alvarez. — First edition.
    pages cm. — (Guardian Herd)
  ISBN 978-0-06-228609-3 (hardcover)
  1. Animals, Mythical—Juvenile fiction. 2. Responsibility—Juvenile fiction.
3. Adventure stories. [1. Fantasy. 2. Animals, Mythical—Fiction. 3. Responsibility—Fiction. 4. Adventure and adventurers—Fiction.] I. Title.
PZ7.A4797St 2015   2014030711
[Fic] 813.6—dc23   CIP
                                                                          AC

15 16 17 18 19   CG/RRDH   10 9 8 7 6 5 4 3 2 1

First Edition

FOR NICK, THE BEST OF BOTH OF US

TABLE OF CONTENTS

Though my soul may set in darkness,
it will rise in perfect light;
I have loved the stars too fondly
to be fearful of the night.

—Sarah Williams, *The Old Astronomer (To His Pupil)*

 RIVER HERD

The black foal:
STAR—solid black with black feathers, white star on forehead

Under-stallions
THUNDERSKY—dark-bay stallion with vibrant crimson feathers, black mane and tail, wide white blaze, two hind white socks. Previously Thunderwing, over-stallion of Sun Herd

HAZELWIND—buckskin stallion with jade feathers, black mane and tail, big white blaze, two white hind socks

SUMMERWIND—handsome palomino pinto stallion with violet feathers

ICERIVER—older dark-silver stallion with powder-blue feathers, white mane, white ringlet tail, blue eyes, white star on forehead. Sire of Lightfeather. Previous over-stallion of Snow Herd

GRASSWING—crippled palomino stallion with pale-green feathers, flaxen mane and tail, white blaze, one white front sock. Deceased

Medicine Mare:

SWEETROOT—old chestnut pinto with dark-pink feathers, chestnut mane and tail, white star on forehead

Mares:

SILVERLAKE—council-mare. Light-gray with silver feathers, white mane and tail, four white socks. Previously Silvercloud, lead mare of Sun Herd

CRYSTALFEATHER—small chestnut mare with bright-blue feathers, two front white socks, white strip on face

DAWNFIR—spotted bay mare with dark-blue and white feathers, black mane and tail

ROWANWOOD—blue roan mare with dark-yellow and blue feathers, white mane and tail, two hind white socks

DEWBERRY—battle mare. Bay pinto with emerald feathers, black mane and tail, thin blaze on forehead, two white hind anklets

LIGHTFEATHER—small white mare with white feathers, white ringlet tail, white mane. Star's dam. Born to Snow Herd, adopted by Sun Herd. Deceased

MOSSBERRY—elderly light-bay mare with dark-magenta feathers, black mane and tail, crescent moon on forehead and white snip on nose, two white hind anklets. Deceased

Yearlings:

MORNINGLEAF—elegant chestnut filly with bright-aqua feathers, flaxen mane and tail, four white socks, amber eyes, wide blaze

BUMBLEWIND—friendly bay pinto colt with gold feathers tipped in brown, black mane and tail, thin blaze on face

ECHOFROST—sleek silver filly with a mix of dark and light purple feathers, white mane and tail, one white sock

BRACKENTAIL—big brown colt with orange feathers, brown mane and tail, two hind white socks

FLAMESKY—red roan filly with dark-emerald and gold feathers

⤚ MOUNTAIN HERD ⤙

ROCKWING—over-stallion. Magnificent spotted silver stallion with dark-blue and gray feathers, black mane and tail highlighted with white, one white front anklet

BIRCHCLOUD—lead mare. Light bay with green feathers, two white front socks

HEDGEWIND—flight instructor. Bay stallion with gray feathers, black mane and tail, thin white blaze

FROSTFIRE—captain. White with violet-tipped light-blue feathers, dark-gray mane and tail, and one blue eye. Born to Snow Herd, adopted by Mountain Herd

SHADEPEBBLE—yearling. Heavily spotted exotic silver filly with pale-pink feathers, black mane and tail, thin blaze, and three white socks. Born a dud and a runt

LARKSONG—sky herder. Buckskin mare with dark-blue feathers, white snip on nose, black mane and tail

DARKLEAF—sky herder. Dun mare with black dorsal stripe, purple feathers, black mane and tail, white snip on nose, golden eyes

SNOW HERD

TWISTWING—over-stallion. Red dun stallion with olive-green feathers, black mane and tail

PETALCLOUD—lead mare. Power-seeking gray mare with violet feathers, silver mane and tail, one white sock, wide blaze on face

CLAWFIRE—captain. White stallion with blue-gray feathers, jagged scar on face, gold eyes

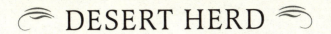 DESERT HERD

SANDWING—over-stallion. Proud palomino stallion with dark-yellow feathers, wide white blaze, one white sock

RAINCLOUD—legendary mare. Fine-boned palomino. Deceased

JUNGLE HERD

SMOKEWING—over-stallion. Speckled bay with brown and white spotted feathers, black mane and tail, white snip on nose

SPIDERWING—legendary over-stallion. Deceased

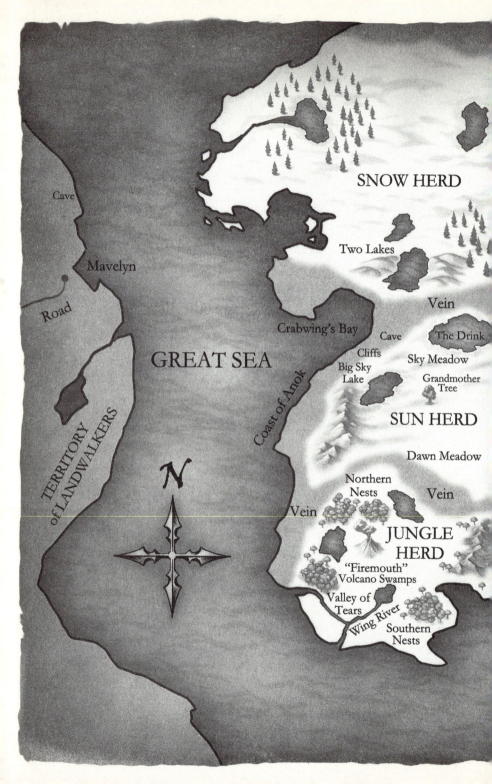

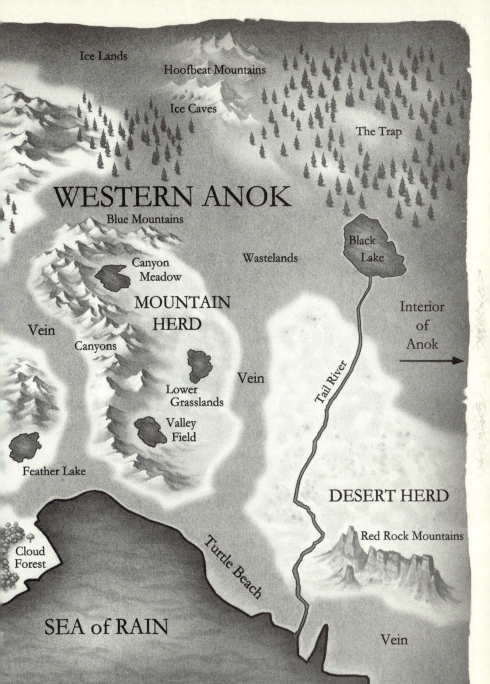

1

INTRUDER

STAR KICKED OFF THE GRASS AND FLEW INTO THE currents on the tail of Hazelwind, four stallions, and two battle mares. The sky was clear, and Star found it difficult to judge his altitude without the clouds. He was a good flier now, but he was still getting used to his powerful wings and to the confusing perspective of the heights. He glanced upward, wanting to soar higher, but Hazelwind leveled out when the air grew thin.

Star glanced at the fliers around him, noticing their chests expanding and falling too fast, their bodies shivering, and their eyes leaking tears. This was high enough for them, but the starfire he'd received a moon ago on his first birthday filled his belly, pulsing through him and warming him, and Star had no trouble breathing. He tamped down his longing to fly higher and focused instead on the mission.

"Eyes down," Hazelwind neighed over the ripping currents. Hazelwind's dam was Silverlake, the past lead mare of Sun Herd, and she'd asked her adult colt to patrol the skies. They circled above the Vein where their herd lived and grazed. Earlier, Hazelwind had spotted the hoofprints of an intruder, and he'd invited Star and some others to help him search for the stranger.

"You're sure we're not looking for a horse," whinnied Dewberry, a small but fierce battle mare. She was four years old and Star didn't know her well, but Hazelwind did. They'd met in Sun Herd's old army.

Hazelwind flicked his ears at her. "Horses don't travel alone."

"Neither do pegasi," she countered.

Hazelwind snorted, and his wing caught the edge of a wind current, sending his body into a spiraling roll. Dewberry nickered in delight as Hazelwind struggled to right himself. When he was gliding safely again, he explained. "A lone horse wouldn't come so close to us, Dewberry, but a spy would."

"A horse spy?" she asked, blinking her large eyes.

Hazelwind opened his mouth to answer, but Dewberry darted ahead, flicking her tail at him.

Star nickered, amused by the banter between the steeds and feeling joyful to be part of a herd and, more than that, to be flying. After Star received his power from the Hundred Year Star, he'd settled his followers in the Vein along the western coast of Anok, near Crabwing's Bay. He called them River Herd in honor of the deep, winding waterway that had led them from the heart of Mountain Herd's territory to the sea.

Five hundred steeds had followed Star out of Rockwing's Canyon Meadow and into an unknown future. Since then, two hundred more had abandoned their herds, risking execution from their over-stallions, to join Star. They had been surviving in the Vein for the last moon, but Star knew he had to find them a home, and quickly. The pregnant mares were nervous and impatient. Some longed to return to Sun Herd's lands, but Star chose not to claim his old territory. It was surrounded by herds that were hostile to him and to the steeds who'd joined him. War could not be avoided if they returned there.

And Star wanted a new beginning for River Herd, a territory unscathed by battle and the devastating memories of the past. But the decision was not his alone, for he was not the over-stallion of River Herd, and neither was Thunderwing. The mighty crimson-feathered bay had given up his power when he followed Star, and he was now known as Thundersky. Star had formed a council to govern River Herd. They met daily to discuss their future, and Star trusted that an appropriate home would be decided upon soon.

In the meantime, River Herd lived peacefully in the Vein, but trouble it seemed had found them.

Star and the others scanned the terrain far below their hooves. The great river that had led them to the coast was just a thin blue line, the trees were shapeless green clumps, and the grazing River Herd pegasi were the size of ants. Star squinted his eyes, and things became clearer. He could make out the colors of the pegasi, even spotting Morningleaf's aqua feathers. From there he surveyed the terrain, sectioning it into shapes so he wouldn't miss anything.

Suddenly a movement caught Star's eye, so stealthy he might have imagined it. He blinked, shaking his head.

"Did you see something?" asked Hazelwind.

"I thought so, but I can't be sure."

The patrol tensed, and Dewberry spoke. "Trust your eyes, Star."

He had seen movement, and she was right; he shouldn't doubt his own eyes. "Yes, I saw something."

"Take us to it," Hazelwind said, ears pinned.

Star curled his wings, held them tight, and plunged headfirst. The eight others followed, plummeting toward land like diving hawks. Star narrowed his eyes against the sharp wind, his teeth rattling and his wings shaking as he sliced through the crosscurrents, picking up speed. The curve of the horizon flattened as the ground raced toward him, ready to slam into him, but everything also became clearer, easier to see. The individual rocks, the leaves, and the thing that had trotted across his vision, its color blending so it was almost invisible. With another sudden movement, the figure appeared in sharp relief. "It's a puma," Star whinnied.

"I see it," said Hazelwind.

The big tawny cat was stalking a small palomino year-ling who had drifted away from the herd to graze on fresh grass. Star whistled a warning to her.

"No!" Hazelwind neighed to Star, but it was too late.

Star's throat tightened as he watched the palomino react to his warning. She spread her wings to fly away but only made it several feet up in the air before the leaping puma's claws sank into her feathers. The cat dragged her to the ground, and within seconds it had its jaws around her throat.

Hazelwind hurtled past Star and rammed the big cat. The stallion, the palomino, and the puma tumbled across the grass. Star and the others landed, surrounding Hazelwind. Dewberry kicked the puma until it let go of the yearling, who then raced away on hoof, her injured wings fluttering behind her. The big cat backed toward the trees, hissing and spitting, then turned and ran.

Star was confused and shocked. "I'm sorry," he said. He would have to do better to protect his herd.

Hazelwind landed and folded his wings. "Movement attracts cats, Star. We had time to reach the yearling before the puma attacked her, but once she bolted, it had to act." Hazelwind took a deep breath. "But don't be upset. You spotted the creature, and that ultimately saved the palomino's life. You did well. Let's go see how she is."

Star and the patrol returned to River Herd. The medicine mare was already tending the palomino, packing her wounds with leaves. "Would you like my help?" Star asked her. He hadn't healed anyone since he'd brought Morningleaf back to life on his birthday.

Sweetroot shook her head. "The fangs just grazed her. She's sore and she lost some hair and feathers, but it's nothing my herbs can't cure."

The palomino yearling, a refugee from Desert Herd, was trembling. "We don't have cats where I live," she said, tossing her mane. "I mean . . . where I used to live."

Star remembered the night this filly arrived. She'd escaped with her family, but her parents and siblings had been caught and killed by Desert Herd warriors. She'd only survived because she'd gone to a river to drink and the patrol hadn't seen her. When she arrived in the Vein, she was almost dead with exhaustion and terror.

Star's wings sagged with sorrow. He looked at Sweetroot, who'd been treating his wounds and counseling him since the day he was born. "This is my fault. We need an army."

Sweetroot nickered. "Calm yourself, Star. Armies are for war."

"But the herd needs protection."

"Protection and war are two very different things."

"Are they?" Star drew up his wings and trotted away, more confused than ever. What sort of black foal was he if his herd wasn't safe even from cats? Thundersky would never have let a cat near his herd.

As Star walked, he felt the questioning eyes of the others on him, so he cantered into the sky where he could think.

He soared through the clouds, glancing down to see

Hazelwind's patrol meeting with River Herd's council of leaders to discuss the puma. Star worried that they hadn't spotted the hooved intruder since the attack. He or she was either hiding very well or had left. Star cruised just over the trees and was not surprised when his best friend, Morningleaf, appeared beside him. They flew together in silence, and after a while his breathing slowed and his thoughts calmed. Finally he broke the silence. "I don't know what I'm doing."

Morningleaf nickered. "Of course you don't; you're a yearling."

"But I'm the black foal. They expect me to know things, to save them. What was I thinking starting a new herd? We don't have a territory or an army. It's winter, and we should be flying south by now, but I don't know where to go."

Morningleaf angled her aqua feathers and banked right. Star followed her. "The council will find us a home, Star. Remember Mossberry's stories—about the ancient pegasi who lived in the interior, on the windy plains? If those lands truly exist, they're not in use. My mother told me we might move there."

Star remembered Mossberry's stories well. She was an elder mare who'd befriended him on his first migration. Neither she nor Star could fly so they migrated with the walkers, and Mossberry had entertained him with stories and legends about the pegasi. A violent forest fire had taken her life on that journey, and Star shuddered at the memory. He looked at Morningleaf. "I remember hearing about the interior of Anok, but we have pregnant mares. We can't waste time traveling to land that may not be habitable."

Morningleaf glanced at him. "Don't worry so much. Things will work out—for the best." Her amber eyes were soft, unconcerned. Her trust in him surpassed reason, but it calmed him too. She dropped and landed in a clearing surrounded by fir trees. Star touched down beside her. "Look at all this sweet, untouched grass," she said.

They lowered their heads and grazed, enjoying the winter sun on their feathers. Before long, rustling leaves drew Star's attention toward the woods. He pricked his ears as a shape creeped through the shadows. Slowly it walked toward them, and every muscle in Star's body tensed. Morningleaf reacted too, lifting her wings, poised for flight. They each froze, listening. Then the shadowy creature stepped into the light. Star's gut dropped, and Morningleaf sucked in her breath.

There, standing in front of them was Brackentail— the Betrayer. The orange-feathered colt said the last two words Star expected to hear. "Help me."

2

THE BETRAYER

STAR AND MORNINGLEAF STOOD ROOTED TO THE ground. They stared at the brown yearling colt who had helped Rockwing plan his battle against Sun Herd only a moon ago, a battle that resulted in many deaths, including Star's mentor, Grasswing. As Brackentail staggered closer, Star and Morningleaf each took a step back, training their eyes on him.

"Please, help me," Brackentail repeated, wheezing as though he had holes in his lungs.

Star scanned the yearling's body. Brackentail was thin and covered in dried blood. His eyes were swollen, almost shut; his tail was chewed to shreds; half his mane had been pulled out; and he had a broken wing.

The orange-feathered limb hung to the ground and had clearly been dragged over weeds and bushes for a long distance. The end feathers were torn, and the longest ones were missing, yanked out by their roots. The healthy wing rested on Brackentail's back. Flies infested his wounds and crawled over his face as though the colt were already dead. "What happened to you?" Star asked.

Brackentail lowered his head. "Rockwing banished me from Mountain Herd the day after you received your power. He said he couldn't trust a betrayer."

Morningleaf snorted. "I'll agree with that."

Brackentail continued. "His captain, Frostfire, escorted me to the Vein, and . . ." He paused, then exhaled long and slow. "He kicked me, broke my wing, and left me to die."

Morningleaf stamped her hoof. "You don't expect us to feel bad about that, do you?"

"Morningleaf!" Star glanced at her, surprised to see her amber eyes crackling with anger.

"No," Brackentail answered her. "I deserved it for what I did." He raised his head, and the slits of his eyes glistened with tears. "But Rockwing lied. I didn't help him win the war. I . . . I wouldn't do that, Morningleaf." He looked directly at the filly, his eyes pleading. "I knew

Silverlake was holding meetings at the waterfall. I knew she was going to try to save the black foal." Brackentail nodded toward Star. "I believed he was dangerous. I was trying to save Sun Herd, and all the pegasi of Anok, from him."

Morningleaf whinnied sharply, her feathers vibrating. "That's no excuse! You should have spoken to my sire, not to Rockwing." Morningleaf charged forward, eye to eye with the brown colt. "Do you know how many Sun Herd pegasi died in the battle?"

Brackentail shrank away from her.

"Their blood is on your wings *forever*!" Morningleaf stamped away from him, breathing fast and hard.

"It wasn't planned," whinnied Brackentail. "I was captured."

Morningleaf whirled on him, teeth bared. "So you betrayed your herd to save yourself?"

Brackentail's thin-slit eyes widened slightly.

"Brackentail," Star interrupted. "You're making things worse. Just tell us why you're here. What do you want?"

Brackentail stared up at the clouds drifting overhead. "I have nowhere else to go."

"So you want to join River Herd?"

The colt nodded.

"No," whinnied Morningleaf. "Absolutely not."

Star touched her back with his wing. Her entire body was trembling. "We'll bring it to the council and let them decide."

She faced him. "You can't be serious."

"If we leave him here, he'll die."

Morningleaf pinned her ears. "That's not our problem."

"He's asking for our protection. And look at him; he's harmless."

"He's harmless *now*, but he helped Rockwing destroy us, and he didn't do anything to protect Echofrost." Star knew that. Echofrost was Morningleaf's friend, and when Brackentail tried to kill Star in a canyon run moons ago, Mountain Herd steeds had captured her and Brackentail. The brown colt worked with his captors, giving them information about Sun Herd, while poor Echofrost had been tortured and then released.

Morningleaf reared, charging Brackentail again, halting just short of ramming him. "Everything you feared Star would do to Sun Herd—*you* did!"

Brackentail collapsed under her accusations. "Kill me then. Please. Just end my life."

Morningleaf's trembling subsided, and she backed away from the yearling colt. She looked at Star. "Do what you want. I won't stop you. But think about how the others will react." She turned and kicked off, flying alone back to River Herd.

Star sighed and approached the brown colt, his lip curling at the stench of his infected flesh and filth. "Can you walk a bit farther?" Star asked him, still unsure what to think about Brackentail's return. He should be feeling joy—his tormentor was now the tormented—but Star felt only sadness. He knew what it was like to be alone, unable to fly, and unwanted by any herd. Star sighed again, shaking his head. He would do what he could to help Brackentail.

"Yes, I can walk," said Brackentail. "Thank you."

"Don't thank me yet. I don't know what the herd will decide to do with you."

Brackentail raised his head. "What do you mean, *decide*? Aren't you the over-stallion?"

Star folded his wings. "No. River Herd has a council, and all decisions are made by them. And it will be difficult for you when you arrive. Prepare yourself."

Brackentail exhaled, looking relieved yet still frightened. The two pegasi walked side by side, like horses, through the lightly wooded terrain toward River Herd.

3

MEMORIES

WHEN STAR AND BRACKENTAIL ARRIVED IN River Herd's main grazing field, a flat meadow dotted with oak trees, they found the pegasi lined up and waiting, their wings flared and their tails swishing angrily. It was clear Morningleaf had already informed them about Brackentail's return. Silverlake stood in the front of the line, watching them, but glanced often toward Hazelwind, whose expression was twisted with rage.

As Star and Brackentail approached, Brackentail's legs quivered, and Star felt his own gut lighten, like he was flying, or falling. He'd faced the hatred of a herd before, and now, even though it was directed at Brackentail, it was all too familiar.

Silverlake shaded her eyes from the bright sun and pricked her ears. "Where did you find him?"

"In a clearing through those woods," Star said, nodding toward the small forest to the southeast.

"Is he the intruder we've been searching for?"

"I think so." Star turned to Brackentail. "How long have you been watching us?"

"Three days," said the colt in a bare whisper.

Hazelwind flew behind Brackentail and inspected the yearling's small hoofprints. "Yes, he's the pegasus I've been tracking."

"He has no herd," said Star. "He's asking for our protection."

Most of the River Herd steeds had once belonged to Sun Herd, so they knew the story of Brackentail's betrayal—they had lived it. And the unusual tale had spread quickly across Anok; even the refugees had heard it. Pegasi never betrayed their herds. All the gathered steeds stared at the brown colt and grumbled with ears pinned.

"He betrayed his herd."

"We lost our land."

"He's not welcome here."

Silverlake let them speak, and then she stepped forward and raised her wings. "The council will meet to discuss Brackentail's fate."

The River Herd steeds respected Silverlake. After Thundersky had banished her, she'd spied on Rockwing and was able to warn Sun Herd about the war before it started, saving them from a worse massacre. They folded their wings and listened to her words now. Silverlake spoke to Brackentail. "You will be placed under guard for our safety, and yours." Then she turned to the medicine mare. "Sweetroot, will you tend to his wounds?"

Sweetroot nodded. Hazelwind rounded up a few stallions to guard Brackentail, and then River Herd went back to grazing and settling in for the evening.

After Brackentail was ushered away, Echofrost cantered forward with her twin brother, Bumblewind, and Morningleaf following her. She slid to a halt in front of Star, whipping her thin tail from side to side. Her expression was haggard, her eyes haunted. "How could you bring him here?"

Star hesitated, then said, "I didn't bring him here. I found him. He's been walking for almost a moon to find us."

"You *know* what I mean," she whinnied. "He tried to kill you, Star."

Star bowed his head. "I remember."

The breeze rifled her short mane, and Echofrost shook her head in irritation. "He's dangerous. He has no place here."

Star glanced at the brown colt as he limped away with the stallions, one wing dragging on the grass, his neck hanging low, and his ears drooping. Brackentail was not dangerous, but the herd's hatred of him was. "He can't hurt us anymore," Star said.

Echofrost folded her purple wings over her silver hide, lifted her head, and searched Star's eyes. He returned her stare and saw the horror of her captivity reflected there, crushing her spirit even here, where she was safe.

Since her kidnapping, Echofrost was not the same filly. She didn't speak about her captivity with Mountain Herd, but the evidence of the torture she'd endured showed on her body. Huge chunks of her mane and tail had been yanked out by their roots and were just beginning to grow back. Bite scars lined her neck and flanks, and her eyes were impassive and solid, like stones. It was as if half of Echofrost had died and was buried in Mountain Herd territory.

Star knew she blamed Brackentail for her misery. When the brown colt had tricked Star into the canyon race, he'd lured him into Rockwing's territory. Echofrost, Morningleaf, and Bumblewind had trespassed across the Vein to save Star from Brackentail's deadly game, and that's when they all had been discovered by a Mountain Herd patrol. Echofrost and Brackentail had been captured; Star and the others had escaped.

Star studied Echofrost's devastated expression, wishing he could help her. He'd spoken to Sweetroot about him healing her just a few days ago, but the medicine mare had stopped him. "Echofrost can heal herself," she'd said.

"How?" Star asked.

Sweetroot exhaled, looking almost as old as Mossberry before she died in the fire. "It's not the injuries bothering her, Star. It's the hatred. If you heal her, she won't learn how to forgive." So Star left his friend alone, and Sweetroot mashed roots for Echofrost every morning and every night to calm her nerves.

And now Brackentail's return inflamed Echofrost all over again. Star exhaled, searching for words, but it was Echofrost who broke the silence. "Brackentail should be executed," she said.

Morningleaf gasped. "That's extreme, don't you think?"

Echofrost looked from Star to her friend, and then to her twin brother. "You've all heard me. I have nothing more to say." She kicked off and flew across the meadow to graze by herself.

Star stood with Morningleaf and Bumblewind. "It's not up to me what we do with him," he said.

Morningleaf nuzzled Star, burying her nose in his thick mane. "She knows that, but she looks up to you. Everyone does."

Star closed his eyes. The herd trusted him because he didn't destroy them with the power he'd received, but now they wanted him to protect them. Where was the line between destroying for evil and destroying for good? Didn't each pegasus deserve to be safe, including Brackentail? "I can't take sides," Star muttered under his breath.

"What did you say?" asked Bumblewind.

Star shook his head, opening his eyes. "I'm just thinking too much."

"I know," said Morningleaf. "Let's get out of here and fly. It will clear your head."

"Yes," agreed Bumblewind. Star's two friends kicked off and soared away. "Hurry, Star, before it's dark."

Star galloped into the sky, savoring the sweet, fluttering thrill that tickled his gut when his hooves lifted off the soil and he was aloft and rising, feeling free. He soared west toward the beach and quickly caught up to his friends, gliding right behind Morningleaf. She turned her head, her amber eyes glittering in the sun. "Are you following me?"

Star ran his eyes over her glossy coat and shining feathers. She was a typical yearling filly, lean and small, but her expression was defiant and amused. "Why would I?" he asked, pricking his ears.

She snorted, teasing him. "You follow me everywhere I go, like when we were foals."

He narrowed his eyes. "I think it was *you* who used to follow *me*."

Morningleaf whinnied over the forceful breeze. "Someone had to keep an eye on you." The three friends crested the cliffs and dived toward the cool ocean.

"Is that right?" Star nickered, flexing his impressive wings; his muscles rippling across his chest. "You still think I can't take care of myself?"

She nodded, her eyes sparkling, and then she veered right and reached her top speed, cruising just over the tops of the waves, her legs tucked tight against her belly.

Star darted after her, his eyes scanning the water for danger. Morningleaf was correct; he did follow her everywhere, and he didn't like her out of his sight. When he closed his eyes each night, memories of her death a moon ago assailed him. He saw her feathers floating and her twisted, broken body, and he felt again the lurching collapse of his heart and how his entire world had shrunk and then shattered when she took her final breath. He needed to keep her safe, even though deep down he feared it would one day destroy him. But he couldn't turn it off, and maybe worse, he didn't want to.

Star circled Morningleaf, dipped toward the sea, and then splashed her as she winged past him.

She squealed and looped around him, making him dizzy. Then she splashed him back, and he tasted the salt of the sea. Bumblewind glided down from the heights to join them.

Morningleaf flew a wide circle around her friends, her eyes bright. "Let's pretend Star's a Jungle Herd stallion on a trading mission with Desert Herd, and we've captured him," she nickered to Bumblewind.

Star let his friends grab his wings and land him on the beach. No longer weanlings but not yet adults, they played for hours. And Star was grateful to Morningleaf for trying to distract him and clear his head, but his troubles weren't so easily vanquished.

Star shivered as a cool coastal breeze blew through his tail. The days were shorter and colder. If they didn't migrate soon, their coats would thicken further, like the Snow Herd steeds in the north, and then they'd be stuck with the heavy pelts until spring.

After a while they grew tired and relaxed on the coarse

sand, cracking crabs for the birds. Morningleaf tossed pieces of meat, nickering happily as the screeching birds caught them, swallowed them midair, and then begged for more with their insistent black eyes and sharp squawks.

"They get lazy if you feed them too much," Star warned his friends. Feeding the birds was bittersweet for him. It reminded him of Crabwing, a seabird he'd befriended when he was hiding on the coast, waiting for his birthday. Star had taken to cracking open crabs and oysters for the little gull, and they had become fast friends. Star had marveled when the bird gave up flying to spend all his time with Star, riding on his back and demanding more food. The gull was content, and he'd trusted Star with his life. Star exhaled. That had been Crabwing's mistake. When Star's enemy Snakewing discovered Star's hiding place and saw him feeding the bird, he'd crushed Star's friend with one swift blow.

Star's thoughts turned to the pegasi of Anok who still wanted to kill him and to those who risked their lives to follow him. Almost every day, refugees from the other herds snuck away from their over-stallions to find Star, seeking a new life, one without war and fear, a life they hoped the black foal could give them. Others never made it. The survivors told awful tales of predators and executions when they finally arrived, exhausted and hungry.

"Let's head back," Morningleaf nickered. Star was jolted from his thoughts. Behind her the sky glowed orange and pink as the sun appeared to sink into the ocean.

"Good idea." Star kicked off and led his friends back to where River Herd was grazing. As they left the coast, a deep and menacing chill suddenly ran through his body. This horrible coldness had been attacking Star ever since he received his power, and his eyes were drawn westward, to the world of the Landwalkers across the Great Sea, each time it occurred. He felt it now as he flew with his friends.

But it was not just a feeling, it was a force. It swept through him, darkening his thoughts, stealing his hope, crushing his joy, and sparking the fire of the Hundred Year Star that burned in the depths of his belly. It made him think of Nightwing the Destroyer, the first black foal to receive the starfire four hundred years ago, and the feeling was becoming harder to ignore. Did the starfire they'd each inherited bind them in some way—like the blood that connected brothers? If Nightwing was hibernating in the west, as Mossberry had suspected, was the dark stallion now awake? Star shook his head as he led his friends to the inland fields.

The farther Star flew from the sea, the faster the

feeling subsided, and as always, he hoped he'd imagined it.

"I'm going to check on Echofrost," Bumblewind said as they approached River Herd. He veered off, found his twin sister, and landed beside her.

Star and Morningleaf settled in the soft grass. "I think it took great courage for Brackentail to approach us," said Star.

"Or great stupidity," said Morningleaf with a snort. She tucked her nose into her aqua feathers.

Star curled into his long black wings, drawing them close to his body, and the two friends drifted into silence. Much had changed in a moon, but even more had not. The pegasi who didn't believe in Star were more afraid of him than ever. The Hundred Year Star was gone from the sky, but in its place was Star himself, the black foal of Anok, the most powerful pegasus alive.

4

CONFLICTED

THE FOLLOWING MORNING STAR MET WITH THE council, which consisted of Silverlake, Thundersky, Hazelwind, Sweetroot, a mare called Dawnfir, and the past over-stallion of Snow Herd, Icewing, who was now Iceriver. "Our coats are growing thick," Silverlake said, speaking first. "It's past time to migrate south, where it's warmer."

"What about Brackentail? We must address his presence here," Hazelwind said. "Echofrost wants him executed, and I agree."

Thundersky raised his head, commanding their attention. "The Betrayer can't be trusted. I don't think we should execute him, but I don't think we should bring him with us when we head south. Let's leave him to his fate."

There was silence as they all considered the options. Silverlake turned to the medicine mare. "If we were to keep the colt, is he well enough to migrate?"

Hazelwind stamped his hoof at the suggestion, but he let Sweetroot answer. The old mare considered her words thoughtfully. "He's not well, but don't underestimate his determination. He shouldn't have made it this far. Something is driving him to survive. Just this one night of rest and grazing has restored him more than I expected. He might keep up if we walked."

"Or Star could heal him," said Silverlake, "and then we could fly."

"No!" neighed Hazelwind. "He must endure the wounds he's earned. If you won't kill him, then leave him here as Thundersky suggested. We'll see how his will to survive handles a pack of wolves or a hungry bear."

Silence fell on the council once again, and soon the steeds were all looking at Star. "Brackentail tried to kill you when he tricked you into the canyon run," Hazelwind reminded Star. "What do *you* want to do with him?"

Star swiveled his ears, thinking. "I want to bring him with us."

Hazelwind snorted and lashed his tail.

"Why?" asked Dawnfir, who had been quiet until now.

"How could you want that after what he did to you and Sun Herd?"

Star saw himself reflected in the dark eyes of his friends. With his head up, he towered over all of them, except the old Snow Herd steed Iceriver. Star appeared a stallion, though he was only a yearling. He understood why they thought he knew what he was doing—he looked like a pegasus leader—but Star was unsure. And now, with them pressing him, he had only one answer and it came from his gut, not his head. "I want to bring him with us because he asked us to."

The pegasi were stunned for a moment. Then Hazelwind, looking baffled, said, "That's ridiculous."

Star shrugged his heavy wings. "I understand why Brackentail wanted me dead. He thought he was protecting Sun Herd and Anok. So did Thundersky." Star glanced at the crimson-winged stallion who'd once promised to execute him. Thundersky sighed deeply, not arguing Star's point. Star continued. "And I don't believe Brackentail walked this far alone with the intent to harm us. He needs us. He's asking for our help and protection, knowing he doesn't deserve it. I think we should give it to him."

"But he caused us to lose our territory," said Thundersky.

"No. Rockwing did that," Star pointed out.

The group shuffled uneasily. Silverlake spoke. "Star is right. Brackentail is not a threat to us anymore."

"I'll never trust him. Ever!" snapped Hazelwind.

Star studied Hazelwind's clenched jaw and noticed how much he resembled his sire when Thundersky was over-stallion of Sun Herd, but Hazelwind had a good point: none of the herd trusted Brackentail. "Why don't we bring him and keep a watch on him," Star suggested. "Give him a chance to earn back our trust."

Hazelwind and the others looked around and nickered. They agreed reluctantly to that condition.

"But what about the migration?" asked Dawnfir. "Because of Brackentail, we'll have to walk, and we're already late. Why don't we travel in two groups: fliers and walkers?"

Silverlake shook her head. "It's not safe to split up; there are too few of us. If we leave today and walk down the coast, we can reach warmer lands within a moon."

"No," said Star. "There's not enough to eat along the coast, and we have pregnant mares ready to give birth any day. If you let me heal Brackentail, we can fly. It will be faster and safer."

"Can you heal just the wing?" asked Hazelwind, his body still tense and angry.

"I don't know; I could try."

The council voted. "Our decision is made. We'll begin our migration today when the sun reaches the peak of the sky, and Star will heal only Brackentail's broken wing."

The council disbanded, and Star trotted directly over to Brackentail, with Sweetroot following. Hazelwind coasted over the grass and landed next to Echofrost. They whispered heatedly and then Echofrost collapsed in a heap. She glared at Star from across the field, her ears pinned and her eyes bright with anger. Star felt terrible for causing Echofrost more pain, but he wouldn't execute Brackentail. He couldn't.

Star focused on his task and halted when he reached the brown yearling. Brackentail was much improved from yesterday, more closely resembling the colt who had tormented Star and his friends the first year of their lives. But now his ears and head were down and humble.

Brackentail cringed when he saw Star. "Have you come to kill me?"

Star touched Brackentail's shoulder with his wing. "No. I've come to heal your wing. You're migrating with us."

"What?" Brackentail blinked his wide eyes. "I am?"

"Yes, but you'll be closely watched. There are those who still don't trust you."

Brackentail nodded and exhaled. His quivering body stilled, but his eyes remained alert.

Star studied Brackentail's wing. It was broken near the root, the worst place for a wing break. It would eventually heal on its own, but it would never support Brackentail's weight in flight again—not without Star's help. Rockwing's captain, Frostfire, had purposefully grounded the yearling for life—turned him into a dud, a punishment almost worse than death.

Star shook his head, tossing his thick mane. He couldn't believe Frostfire's cruelty. Frostfire and Star's mother, Lightfeather, shared the same sire: Iceriver. Star had learned the news from Iceriver himself after he joined River Herd. How could one stallion sire two pegasi who were so different? Perhaps it was the mares who made the difference. Lightfeather's dam had died saving her filly from a bear. Frostfire's dam, Petalcloud, had given her colt away the day he was weaned, selfishly trading him for her own freedom. Now Frostfire, the white stallion with one blue eye, plagued Anok as Rockwing's cruelest captain, famous for his devastating injuries. And even worse: this vicious captain, half brother to Lightfeather, was Star's uncle.

Star shuddered and returned his attention to

Brackentail. Old memories assailed him like freezing gusts of wind: Brackentail calling him a horse, Brackentail mocking his mother, and Brackentail's attempt to kill him in the canyon. Anger followed the memories, and his starfire flamed and coursed through his veins. Star battled a sudden urge to destroy Brackentail, to torch his ruined wing and watch the feathers burn.

"No!" he whinnied, choking on the sudden starfire that filled his lungs and throat. Something was wrong. He scooted backward, away from Brackentail. His body shook, and small silver sparks popped between his teeth.

Half of River Herd galloped into the sky; the other half stared at Star, tensed for flight.

Star trembled violently as the starfire roared through his body. It was cold, and wild—stampeding through his veins, throbbing like it might explode. He dropped his eyes, afraid to look at Brackentail, who cowered in front of him.

Morningleaf darted out of the trees and landed next to Star. "Star! Look at me," she whinnied.

Star faced her as frothy sweat erupted across his chest and dripped to the ground. His hooves danced like those of a frightened land horse.

Morningleaf pressed her aqua wings against his

cheeks, blocking his vision of everything but her. "Star, what's happening?"

"It's the starfire," he whispered, and dark-gray smoke drifted from his mouth.

"You can't heal him?" she asked.

"It's not that. I might kill him."

"What?" Morningleaf pricked her ears. "I don't understand."

Star shook his head, tossing his mane from one side of his neck to the other in a black arc. "Neither do I. I don't want to hurt him, but I'm angry with him. It's not like when I healed you. It feels different."

Morningleaf searched his eyes. "It's your anger, Star. You have to let it go."

Star nodded, grimacing. "I'll try." Morningleaf lowered her wings and Star refocused on Brackentail. The colt had bathed in the sea earlier. He smelled of brine and was free of flies. Brackentail's raw wounds stood in sharp contrast to his clean coat. Jagged gashes crisscrossed his chest and back, swollen skin marked areas of extreme bruising, and his right front leg was sliced open almost to the bone.

It was obvious Frostfire had kicked the colt to near death, but it was the ends of Brackentail's broken wing that captured and held Star's attention. The frayed and bloody feathers, the inability to fly—Star had suffered the same torture. It was something so horrific he wouldn't wish it on his worst enemy. To take away the ability to fly from a pegasus *was* abominable.

Star stared at Brackentail's mangled feathers and saw his own, from when he was a dud. The starfire settled and then rumbled through his belly, radiating a pleasant, tingling sensation across Star's ribs. He drew on this gentle power, letting it swell in his chest, and then he opened his jaws and drenched Brackentail's wing in golden light.

The colt gasped and staggered, steadying himself so he didn't fall over.

Star pushed the starfire up and out, exhaling light and sparkling electricity into Brackentail's orange wing. The yearling's flight bones glowed, appearing as bolts of lightning under his skin, and the starfire vibrated the wing and coursed down through each broken feather.

Around them, River Herd landed and gathered. A hush fell over all of them like the quiet that announced the birth of a new foal.

When the feathered limb was restored, Star closed his mouth. Brackentail stared at his wing, unsure, and then he extended it and flapped it. It was healed, completely.

Star knew he was supposed to stop with the wing, but he saw that Brackentail's leg wound was located across a knee joint. Movement of that leg would repetitively aggravate the wound, and it would never heal. Star quickly blasted the area with a burst of golden fire. He left the rest of the wounds to heal on their own.

When Star turned around, he was face-to-face with Echofrost. Huge, angry tears rolled down her cheeks. She shook her head, turned her back on Star, and walked away. A kick to his gut would have hurt Star less. He staggered into Morningleaf.

The chestnut filly propped up Star with her body. "Echofrost just needs time."

"She hates me," neighed Star.

"She hates Brackentail," argued Morningleaf.

Sweetroot inspected Brackentail's freshly healed wounds. "Can you fly?"

Brackentail flapped his wings and flew a small circle around the meadow. "It feels like it was never broken," he said in amazement. He turned to Star, baffled and awed. "You . . . you saved me, Star."

Star was too confused and sad about Echofrost to speak. He nodded quickly to Brackentail, and then he and Morningleaf kicked off and flew away to graze together before the migration later that day.

"Don't feel bad," said Morningleaf when they landed in a meadow not far from River Herd. "I heard that

Brackentail tried to apologize to Echofrost last night. She wouldn't listen to him, but I think she'll come around, in time. None of this is your fault."

"It feels like my fault. All of it." Star swept his wing, indicating the entire land of Anok.

Morningleaf chuckled. "Remember the things Grasswing told you, Star. There were kidnappings, and wars, and hurt feelings long before you showed up. You blame yourself too much."

"Maybe you're right." Star glanced westward, remembering Grasswing, the wise leader of the walkers. He'd died in Sun Herd's battle against Rockwing, killed by Rockwing himself in a heroic standoff. Star could just glimpse the sea between two hills. The light twinkled on the distant waves like the blue shimmer of Morningleaf's feathers. Star sighed. "Or maybe that's what bothers me. The world hasn't changed, Morningleaf. War and death haven't left the herds. I think the golden meadow is our true home and Anok is the illusion—but one that we must endure."

"Endure?" Morningleaf snorted. "Don't be so gloomy, Star. We can fly!" She kicked off and whinnied to him, "Come on. Let's play one last time before the migration. Catch me if you can!"

5

BLUE TONGUE

STAR WATCHED MORNINGLEAF SHOOT ACROSS the grass, flickering her sassy tail. Several yearlings joined the game of chase. Star followed, angling his wings for speed. Morningleaf darted into the dense coastal forest that surrounded River Herd's temporary grazing lands. She dodged the towering redwood trees and creeping branches, sometimes flying sideways. She tagged a spotted filly and then darted away as the filly gave chase.

Star was too big to follow at such speed. He cruised above the redwood grove, tracking the yearlings from the air and inhaling the musty scent of the forest. The spotted filly darted out of the woods and tagged Star's wing. "You're it!" she whinnied.

Tingling with pleasure at being included, Star tucked his wings and rocketed toward land, flying as low as he could. A bay yearling who was also too large to fly in the trees soared ahead of him. Star flapped hard, surging faster, and gained quickly on the bay, who glanced up when Star's shadow covered him and neighed in surprise. He banked hard, but Star gripped the current and matched the speed of his turn. They rose and whipped over the tree-tops. Star dropped below the colt and then rolled, tagging the bay gently with his hoof. "You're it!" he whinnied.

As the bay chased down another steed, Star circled around and searched for Morningleaf. He glimpsed her red body and big white blaze flashing deep in the forest. She glanced up, saw Star, and squealed, thinking he was still it. She braked, circled, and twisted through the branches until she lost him.

"Morningleaf!" he called.

There was no answer.

"Where are you?" he whinnied.

But there was still no answer from Morningleaf.

Star's gut twisted, and his heart floated in his chest, drifting like a loose feather. He circled the part of the forest where he'd last seen her, squinting his eyes and wishing the bright light of the Hundred Year Star still blazed in the sky.

Then a blur of chestnut darted through a blind of tree needles. "Morningleaf!" He snorted. "I thought I'd lost you."

She whinnied, looking back at Star while she flew. "You'll never lose me, Star."

Suddenly a foreign pegasus swooped in front of Morningleaf, but she was watching Star. "Look out!" Star neighed.

Morningleaf turned her head just in time to see the strange mare before she crashed into her. The two tumbled across the sky. Star trumpeted a loud alarm to River Herd. Morningleaf quickly regained her wings and so did the stranger. They circled each other warily.

Thundersky, Hazelwind, and others from River Herd careened through the branches and surrounded the strange mare. She was white and furry, with yellow feathers and blue eyes, clearly a Snow Herd steed.

Iceriver spoke. "I know her." He hovered and faced his friend. "Are you alone?"

The white mare flapped her wings, out of breath. "I am. I'm a messenger. May I land, please?"

"Of course," said Iceriver. He and Hazelwind escorted the mare back to River Herd's main grazing meadow.

The messenger mare didn't wait for further introductions. She spoke so all could hear. "Plague has struck Snow Herd."

The River Herd steeds reared and immediately backed away from her, frightened.

"I'm not sick," she said. "But I've come to warn you, as is the custom."

Star glanced at Thundersky, who was once criticized by Iceriver for his unwillingness to send messages. Thundersky spoke. "How is it spread?"

The mare folded her pale-yellow-feathered wings. "Through contact, the air, and our droppings. The exposed pegasi who don't contract the plague are carriers of it. The sickness began after Star's birthday. Since then, some members of our herd have snuck off to join your herd, which is why I'm here. If they aren't sick, they are carriers. It's the worst plague I've seen in my lifetime. Anywhere you go, you will leave it in the soil and ruin grazing lands. You *must* isolate yourselves immediately."

"How do we know you're telling the truth?" asked Hazelwind.

The mare flattened her ears, and her voice trembled. "Come see for yourself if you don't believe me. Snow Herd can't stop you. Half of us are already dead." She choked back a sob.

"Thank you," said Iceriver. "You may rest here before you return."

"No. I must leave now. I have more herds to warn."

"Is it like the White Death or Black Hoof?" Sweetroot asked.

The messenger shook her head. "Neither. It's totally new. We call it Blue Tongue." She glanced at the pregnant mares and then said, "Our foals are dying in their mothers' bellies." With that she kicked off and flew east.

The River Herd steeds stared at one another, bewildered and afraid.

Silverlake spoke. "We have to cancel our migration today. If we head south, we could infect Jungle Herd." She looked at her mate, Thundersky. "We can't live in the Vein between the herds. We could infect the land, and we can't stay here where we've eaten almost all the food. We'll have to travel north, to the Ice Lands."

"But who says we're infected?" asked Bumblewind.

Silverlake nodded to Sweetroot, and the old medicine mare spoke. "I've been keeping an eye on three sick refugees, all from Snow Herd. They haven't responded to any of my medicines, and their tongues are blue."

"And you didn't tell us!" whinnied Dewberry, the battle mare who flew patrols with Hazelwind.

Sweetroot lowered her head, looking miserable. "Only Silverlake. I—I didn't understand it, and I've never seen anything like it. The mares are eating and drinking, but they're weak, and their throats ache. I didn't think too much about their blue tongues." Her ears drooped. "They must still be in the early stages, but it's too late for all of us—we've been exposed."

The pregnant mares whinnied in terror, and Morning-leaf glanced at Star. "If the herds ever needed a healer, it's now," she said to him.

"You're right." Star caught Silverlake's eye. "Let's gather the council. I want to travel to Snow Herd's territory to heal them."

Sweetroot pricked her ears. "All of them? You can do that?"

Star flicked his tail. "I don't know. At least I think I can."

Sweetroot huffed, her eyes glittering. She reached out and touched Star's shoulder with her wingtips. "Your power is like a mighty river, Star. Calm on top but ever flowing beneath. Sometimes I forget . . ." Her voice drifted off.

Star dipped his head. "Forget what?"

"That you're fantastic."

6

HIGH FLIGHT

THE FOLLOWING MORNING, THE RIVER HERD steeds gathered together. The council had met the previous night and confirmed the decision to travel north. Star healed the three sick pegasi mares, but he couldn't guarantee they weren't still carrying the disease. All of River Herd could be carrying it by now.

Thundersky spoke to the pegasi. "We'll fly in the Vein, traveling east until we pass Snow Herd's territory, then we'll veer north and head into the Ice Lands. The journey will take five days if we keep our rest stops short and also fly at night."

River Herd understood the reasoning, and none were willing to spread a plague that could wipe out every pegasus in Anok, but they weren't happy about it. The pregnant mares were especially concerned. "What will we eat there?" asked one.

Star knew that Thundersky had flown all over Anok, surviving by himself in the Vein. So had Iceriver and others; it was part of their training for the army. These steeds had warned the council that food in the north was scarce, but the Ice Lands were uninhabited, and there they would not spread the Blue Tongue plague. Thundersky answered the young mother as best he could without alarming her. "We're a small herd, less than a thousand; we'll be able to survive."

Survive? Star shuddered at the word. He wanted more for his herd than mere survival. But he would not be joining them right away in the Ice Lands. He had a visit to make first. He stood on the outskirts of the trampled meadow with Bumblewind, Dewberry, and Morningleaf. "We're ready to depart," he announced to River Herd.

The evening before, Star had gained permission from the council to visit Snow Herd, but not without some arguing. "I can heal them," he'd said. "I'll take a small group with me, so Snow Herd understands we aren't there to fight."

"I'll go with him," volunteered Morningleaf.

"Me too," said Bumblewind. Star had asked his friends

to attend the meeting in the hope they would join him, and they did. Only Echofrost had refused.

"And I'll take Dewberry," said Star. The little mare was scrappy and fearless, but small enough not to appear threatening.

Silverlake flicked her ears, looking concerned. "Twistwing won't welcome you, Star."

Twistwing, who used to be Twistfire from Sun Herd, had openly called for Star's death from the day Star was born. He'd joined Rockwing in attacking Star the night he received his power, and now Twistwing was over-stallion of Snow Herd. Star tossed his long forelock out of his eyes. "No, he won't welcome me, but he won't turn me away. You heard the messenger; half his herd is dead."

Hazelwind dragged his sharpened hoof through the dirt, scratching a deep line in the soil. He pinned his ears at Star but looked at everyone gathered. "Why are we helping our enemy?" he asked, spitting out the words. "If Snow Herd is truly half dead, let's leave them that way. Maybe the rest will die too."

Star cocked his head. He'd never considered *not* helping Snow Herd. He didn't know what to say.

Silverlake answered. "It's worth helping them if it brings peace between River Herd and Snow Herd," she said. "This is an opportunity, Hazelwind."

The stallion snorted. "It's an opportunity wasted. We could end Snow Herd now, while they're weak."

Star braced at Hazelwind's harsh words. The young stallion had once been one of his greatest supporters. Hazelwind believed Star was the healer, but ever since he'd fought in Sun Herd's final battle against Mountain Herd, Hazelwind had changed.

Iceriver spoke, his eyes soft and sad. "It would mean a lot to me, Star, if you healed Snow Herd. They are good steeds, most of them." Iceriver's words floated over all of them, stilling their rustling feathers as they listened.

While Star had some doubts about his grandsire, the ex-over-stallion of Snow Herd had proved helpful and trustworthy. And once Thundersky accepted him, everyone in River Herd had as well. The two stallions were often seen flying together and talking. Star imagined Iceriver was Thundersky's first real friend, and the only other stallion in River Herd who understood the unique trials Thundersky had faced as an over-stallion.

But Iceriver avoided Star, his grandson. Probably because he felt shame for not helping Star's mother when she was driven out of Snow Herd years ago. Star didn't know, and he didn't press the old stallion for answers.

Iceriver had let his filly go without a fight, and nothing could change that, but Star was grateful that Lightfeather had landed in Sun Herd and that he'd been born in Dawn Meadow.

"Maybe Silverlake is right," said Thundersky, breaking the silence. "Maybe Star can form a truce with Twistwing and Snow Herd."

The council had voted, and it was decided. Star and his friends would travel to Snow Herd's territory.

Now Star watched as Silverlake led the migration to the Ice Lands. She cantered into the clouds, her wide wings muscling the wind, with the River Herd steeds following her. They broke into small V formations consisting of twelve to fifteen steeds each. Brackentail coasted behind Thundersky and was closely watched by several burly stallions. He flew well, and all signs of injury to his broken wing were gone.

As the herd soared out of sight, Star turned to his friends. "Ready?"

Bumblewind stretched his wings. "Shouldn't we have a plan, in case things don't go our way?"

"That's not a bad idea," said Dewberry.

"Really, you think so?" Bumblewind puffed up his feathers. Dewberry snorted, ignoring him.

Star and Morningleaf exchanged amused glances.

Dewberry stared pointedly at Star. "Anyway, we have *him*. We don't need to flee from any herd." Her dark eyes sparkled with excitement.

Morningleaf huffed. "That's not a good plan."

"Why not?" asked Bumblewind. "He's got the starfire. You would use it to protect us. Right, Star?"

"Of course," said Star, but he hoped he wouldn't have to.

"All right then," said Bumblewind. "We have our plan. Now, let's fly." He kicked off and Star followed, passing Bumblewind and taking the headwind like he always did. The others coasted on his wide current.

Star flattened his neck and soared over Anok, his heart racing with the thrill of flight. The oversize wings that had plagued his foalhood now carried him effortlessly through the clouds. When he flew, the starfire heated his belly and coursed through his veins, infusing his muscles with energy. He scanned the terrain below, enjoying the heights and the pleasure of being the largest creature in the sky. He whinnied to his friends, his voice whipping behind him, only a whisper on the rippling air currents. "Let's see how high we can go!"

Star lifted his nose and pumped his wings, driving his body into the cloud layer. He peeked back to see his friends following, their eyes glittering with joy. It was much more difficult to fly straight up than it was to cruise parallel to the land, but Star's wings were powerful. He surged higher, his black hide damp with cloud sweat, until he passed out of the mist to where the sun was bright.

He narrowed his eyes against the sharp rays and the chill so penetrating he could feel it in his hooves. He looked down and saw that his friends had flown as high as they could. They circled, watching him and waiting. Morning-leaf was shivering. Star looked up and couldn't resist the urge to try flying higher.

He angled his nose toward the sun and flapped his massive wings. Through the patchy clouds he could see the curve of the horizon, and he marveled at the planet, which was not flat as it appeared on land, but round. Far below his dangling hooves, flocks of birds flew like tiny gnats, rivers were blue lines, and rugged mountain ranges rose like sentinels out of the flat, grassy plains, guarding them from the wind. He hovered, gulping the thin, cold air—and he knew he could fly higher still.

He looked to where the blue sky turned black, to the space where the Hundred Year Star had glowed so brightly only a moon ago, and he yearned to fly there. He pinned his ears against the prickling radiation of the sun, and his lungs burned as though he were running out of air. Star craned his neck, squinting at the edge of the atmosphere, and wondered what it would be like to glide in outer space, where there were no currents and the surroundings were blacker than he. Of course no pegasus could fly among the stars; he knew that, but it didn't stop him from wishing he could.

Star peeked below and saw his friends as mere dots— one brown, one red, and one splotched. His eyes watered, and the edges of his hooves began to melt from the burning power of the sun. This was high enough. Star relaxed his wings and let his body stall in midair. When he began to fall, he flexed his wings, controlling the current, and he rocketed toward his friends, squinting as the crosswinds battered his face. He slowed when he neared them and glided in a large circle.

"You were so high!" whinnied Bumblewind, his teeth chattering.

"A little too high," muttered Morningleaf.

Dewberry's eyes were brilliant. "The legends about the Desert Herd steeds must be true. It's said they can fly as high as you just did, maybe higher."

"I wish Echofrost had seen it," said Bumblewind as the four of them dropped back toward the cloud layer. "She won't believe me when I tell her."

"What's it like up there?" asked Dewberry.

"Hard to breathe," Star answered. "And freezing cold, but hot too." He shook his forelock out of his eyes. "I can't explain it." Star didn't want to encourage them to try it. His friends had flown as high as they safely could.

The group coasted in silence until dusk. The terrain had changed drastically as they flew north. The trees were shorter, the animals larger, and the land more desolate. Patches of snow appeared, and the tall field grasses gave way to stubby weeds. Morningleaf spotted a creek, and they landed to graze, drink, and sleep for the night.

The next morning the four pegasi flew north, continuing their path toward Snow Herd. Within an hour they approached a landscape buried in snow. The wind was cold and unforgiving, reaching deep into their bones. Star was glad their coats had thickened while they were living in the Vein.

"Look there," said Star, nodding toward a frozen oval lake far below them. "Silverlake told me that when we reach the land of frozen lakes, we're in Snow Herd's territory."

Star led his group out of the clouds and straight into a pack of Snow Herd warriors. He gasped, shocked, and his heart thrummed in a fast, steady beat.

"We're definitely in the right place," huffed Dewberry. She coiled her front legs and rattled her feathers at the foreign stallions. Morningleaf and Bumblewind copied her.

"It *is* the black foal," whinnied a light-gray steed as though his group had been watching them for a while. "Seize them!" he neighed to the others.

The warriors surged forward, casting apprehensive glances at Star, and snatched his friends by the wings, dragging them across the sky. A cream-colored stallion trumpeted an alarm to his herd that carried across the snow.

Dewberry kicked her captor in the knees and twisted, trying to yank her wing free of his jaws. "I need backup!" she whinnied.

But Star was already on his way, charging toward her, his jaws clenched. He slammed into the white stallion's chest, and the hit forced him to release Dewberry. The stallion wheezed, gasping for air. Star hadn't planned to fight the Snow Herd stallions, but his gut fluttered with his first small victory.

Suddenly, another warrior came at them, clubbing Star

over the head with his hoof, and Star tumbled into a cloud, scattering the mist, before regaining his wings. Dewberry was free and battling a gray stallion, but Morningleaf dangled from a set of powerful jaws, squealing in anger and pain.

Star's fast breaths filled his ears, and his heart beat wildly against his rib cage. He dived into the flank of the stallion holding Morningleaf and bit into his meaty flesh. They tussled across the sky, a tangle of feathers and legs, until the buckskin stallion finally released Morningleaf, and she darted out of harm's way.

Star and the buckskin faced off, circling each other just below the first layer of clouds. With Morningleaf safe, Star focused on his opponent. Like all Snow Herd stallions, the buckskin was big and heavy, with large, round muscles. His eyes blazed, and if he felt any fear of the black foal, his fury had squashed it.

He lunged at Star, teeth bared. Star dodged him, but the stallion snatched a mouthful of Star's mane and yanked hard, ripping some hair out by the roots. Star braced his wings to keep from tumbling sideways. He kicked at the stallion and missed. The buckskin extended his wings, reared up, and pounded Star's back with his front hooves.

Reeling, Star chomped back his agony and whirled to

face his opponent. They struck each other, chest to chest, but Star's unsharpened hooves couldn't slice through the warrior's skin. Star dived in to bite his throat. The buckskin evaded him and kicked Star, his hooves as sharp as ice, opening wounds in Star's skin.

"Star!" whinnied Morningleaf, panting, but she couldn't help him. She and Dewberry were battling for the release of Bumblewind. The first stallion Dewberry attacked had fled. Star guessed he would return with reinforcements.

"I'm fine," Star neighed. The buckskin squealed in anger and flew forward, ramming Star in the chest again. Star's wings lost their purchase on the wind, and he fell toward land, upside down. The buckskin leaped onto Star's belly and drove him toward the snow, whinnying in triumph. With the stallion's weight on him, Star couldn't flip over.

"Use your starfire!" neighed Bumblewind, who was free now.

The starfire gurgled like lava, ready to explode. But Star didn't want to use it, not this way. He gritted his teeth, threw back his head, and forced his body into a backward nosedive. He plummeted toward a pine forest, out of control but now free of the stallion.

"No!" whinnied Morningleaf, charging after him.

Star's wings whipped in the breeze, and the delicate end-bones threatened to break. Below him, the dense forest of snow-splashed pine trees circled as he fell in a headfirst spiral. He had seconds to pull out of the dive before he crashed. Many moons of swimming in Crab-wing's Bay had strengthened his huge flying muscles. Star drew his wings tight to his body, angled the folded ends into the wind, and then slowly extended the tips, slicing them into the current and gently pushing down, capturing the breeze.

His body evened out just before impact, and he rock-eted through the trees, his hooves skimming the white powder and his body tilting sometimes sideways to avoid slamming into large branches. He tried to control his manic heartbeat as he raced through the forest, which was too narrow for his large body. Trees flashed by faster than he could think, and it was pure instinct that kept him from colliding with them.

Star saw a space open up in the branches and beyond it, blue sky. He lifted his head and rocketed out of the forest, knocking the snow off the pine needles. He angled his wings to slow himself and then soared gracefully to an open clearing where he landed, breathing hard and feeling dizzy. Morningleaf, Bumblewind, and Dewberry landed next to him. "That was incredible," squealed Dewberry.

Sudden fury roiled in Star's gut, and he turned on her. "Why did you attack them?"

She pinned her ears and backed away. "What do you mean?"

"They were going to take us to Twistwing," said Star, shaking his head. "All we had to do was let them."

Dewberry bristled. "Nobody *takes* me, Star. I go under my own power or not at all." She rattled her emerald feathers. "We're clearly not a threat; there was no need for the stallions to use force."

The stallions they spoke of landed next to them. They were wary and also breathing hard. "You can't get away," said the gray one.

"Actually we can," said Star, lashing his tail, his eyes glowing gold. "But we don't want to." He glared at Dewberry. "We flew here on purpose, to help you."

"Help us?" whinnied the buckskin.

Star noticed the stallions he'd attacked were bleeding but were not mortally injured. He was covered in bites and scratches. Morningleaf limped on three legs, and Bumblewind had lost a fair amount of feathers. Dewberry appeared unharmed, but Star was certain his small band of friends would have been slaughtered if the fight had continued much longer. Star looked back at the Snow Herd stallions. "Your messenger told us about the Blue Tongue plague. I can heal your sick steeds." Star swallowed his irritation with Dewberry. "In spite of what just happened, we haven't come to fight."

The gray stallion cocked his head, thinking. Then he said, "Twistwing will decide that. Follow me." He kicked off and flew low over the sparkling snow, with Star and his friends following.

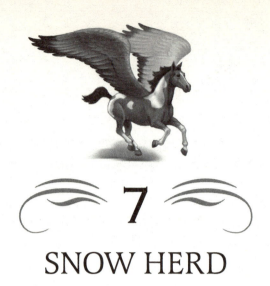

7

SNOW HERD

STAR AND HIS FRIENDS SWOOPED OVER A SET OF low foothills and dropped into a wide valley, the heart of Snow Herd's territory. They cruised just over the terrain, tailing Twistwing's warriors. Two frozen lakes, sparse trees, gray boulders, and patches of turned-up moss decorated the otherwise bland landscape of trampled snow and gray skies. The members of Snow Herd were gathered into four separate groups, probably based on their level of illness, and the herd was small, consisting of maybe eighteen hundred pegasi.

"Where are the dead?" Dewberry asked the warriors.

Morningleaf jerked her head toward the little battle mare, looking appalled, but the buckskin stallion kept flying and answered her question without emotion. "We fly them to the ocean and drop them where the water is deep."

Dewberry nodded, and Star remembered hearing that her mother was the medicine mare who'd trained Sweet-root. Her question wasn't mean-spirited; it was important, because dead bodies continued to spread disease. Star exhaled, feeling sad for Snow Herd's lost pegasi but also hopeful. He could save the rest of them.

The Snow Herd stallions landed them near the healthi-est of the groups. Star recognized Twistwing's olive-green feathers as the over-stallion galloped toward him, followed by a pretty gray mare.

"That's Petalcloud," whispered Morningleaf with a gasp. The mare was a legend, the first foal born alive to Rock-wing and his mate, Birchcloud. But then she'd abandoned them to become lead mare of Snow Herd. When Rockwing demanded she trade her firstborn foal to him as payment for her freedom, she had been happy to agree. She'd sent her colt, Frostfire, away on the day he was weaned. The rest of her foals were born dead, like her sire's.

Petalcloud was young to lead a herd, only seventeen. She was thought to be the most beautiful mare in Anok, although not everyone agreed about that. Star certainly didn't think so, but her beauty was all the more startling since she came from Mountain Herd, the territory where the mares were usually quite plain.

Petalcloud spoke first, gazing at Star, her eyes bright. "The black foal, in the flesh," she nickered, flicking her silky tail at him. Her voice was throaty, with a lilting vibration like the purr of a great cat.

Star shifted uncomfortably, and behind him he heard Morningleaf snort. Petalcloud stepped forward until she was face-to-face with Star. He saw none of the veiled fear in her eyes that most steeds, even some from his own herd, harbored for him. She touched her muzzle to his and breathed softly into his nose, greeting him as though they were old friends. As her guest, Star tolerated it, but he did not trust her.

Twistwing stamped his hoof and spoke to Star. "You're trespassing. Tell me why I shouldn't kill you now?"

Irritated, Star threw his head up, displaying his full height, and Petalcloud backed away from him. "I've come to heal your sick pegasi, to rid your herd of Blue Tongue."

Some members of Snow Herd overheard Star, and they passed the message along in excited whispers. Petalcloud swiveled her ears, listening, then she gave Twistwing an almost imperceptible shake of her head. He stared at his mate for a long while, and it was like they spoke without words, but the mare's tense body revealed her feelings. She was hostile to the idea.

Twistwing broke the silence, speaking to Star. "We're recovering from Blue Tongue. We don't need your help."

Dewberry huffed, glancing around the valley. "Recovering? I count six hundred of you right now with advanced symptoms: rapid breathing, cloudy eyes, and lost weight." She nodded toward a group of pegasi lying on their sides. "And those two hundred over there will be dead by morning. The rest of you have been exposed. You aren't *recovering* from it; you're *succumbing* to it."

"Are you a medicine mare?" asked Petalcloud, her voice sharp.

"No," admitted Dewberry, "but my mother was."

"Enough of us are immune to survive this."

Dewberry pinned her ears, pointing her wing at a group of mares. "Half those foals will be born dead. Star can save them." She spoke loud enough for all the Snow Herd steeds to hear her.

Petalcloud swished her tail. "Foals are born dead all the time."

"Maybe yours and your father's, but not most," quipped Dewberry.

Petalcloud squealed sharply and lunged at Dewberry. Star shoved his way between the mares, taking their bites to his own flesh and pushing them apart with his great wings.

"Enough!" roared Twistwing. Petalcloud backed away, making a hissing noise in the back of her throat, her neck and ears flat, and her tail lashing violently.

Star pushed Dewberry into Bumblewind. "Hold her," he said. Bumblewind wrapped his wings around the battle mare's chest, and Morningleaf positioned herself in front. Dewberry pawed the snow but stayed.

Twistwing and Star faced each other. Star pricked his ears, taking in all of Snow Herd. He believed Dewberry and Petalcloud were both correct. Snow Herd had succumbed to Blue Tongue, but they would survive it in the end. There were enough immune pegasi to rebuild the herd, but they would be weakened by their losses for many years to come. If they accepted his help, they would be better off.

Twistwing sighed and then spoke. "Since you're not a raiding party, you may leave without harm, if you go right now."

Star arched his neck, stunned. "But I can help you. I can save the foals and stop the threat of the plague spreading to the other herds."

"No. You will leave."

Behind Twistwing, Snow Herd grumbled.

"Let him stay."

"He's the healer."

"He brought the blue-winged filly back from the dead. He can help us."

"I don't understand. You would let your steeds die?" Star asked, perplexed.

Twistwing pinned his ears. "Rather than take help from the black foal? Yes."

A pregnant mare whinnied in anger and charged Twistwing. His stallions blocked her, biting the top of her neck until she squealed in pain and submitted to them. Twistwing turned around, baring his teeth, and addressed his confused and frightened herd. "Do you know what it means to accept his help?" he asked, his words carrying far across the frozen land, silencing everyone. "Who of you would stand against him if he chose to conquer us, to take over Snow Herd? We will owe him—forever. He will heal us, but inflict a direr wound upon us: servitude to his whims."

The Snow Herd pegasi trembled, unsure.

"That's not true! I don't want Snow Herd," whinnied

Star. He exchanged a disbelieving look with Morningleaf. She shrugged her wings, as baffled as he.

"You say that now," said Twistwing, rearing and flapping his olive-green wings. "I won't make a pact with the black foal."

Star clenched his jaw. By using the word *pact*, Twistwing purposefully reminded his herdmates of Nightwing. Desert Herd had sought to make a pact with the Destroyer four hundred years ago—but the result was the near extinction of all pegasi when Nightwing refused the deal.

"He's come to conquer us!" whinnied a yearling colt, and the healthiest steeds in the herd stampeded into the gray sky, away from Star. Petalcloud arched her neck and stared him down, looking fearless and triumphant both at once.

Twistwing's warriors rushed to his side, and they all faced Star. "Leave us," the over-stallion commanded.

"Come on. Let's go," said Morningleaf, nudging Star. "There's nothing we can do for this herd."

Still baffled, Star nodded and kicked off, flying out of the valley. His friends followed, riding his wake, all of them silent. Star cruised across the foothills to an open expanse of land consisting of miles and miles of snow. There were no trees or rocks, and only the occasional lake.

Star oriented himself using the movement of the sun as his guide and traveled northeast, toward the Ice Lands of Anok, where River Herd waited for him.

"I don't understand it," Star said to Morningleaf, who flew next to him. "Why won't they let me help them?"

She sighed. "They don't trust you."

"But I didn't bring an army to threaten them." He gazed at his wounds. "It was the opposite. *They* attacked *me*."

Morningleaf flattened her neck against the biting wind. "You don't need an army to kill pegasi, Star. You're the black foal."

"But I told them I wouldn't hurt them, and I didn't use my starfire."

Morningleaf glanced at him, her amber eyes flat and sad. "I know, and they heard you, but they weren't really listening."

A hard lump formed in Star's throat, and he dropped the conversation.

At dusk they landed for the night. "I'll take the first watch," said Star.

"No. You're injured. I'll do it," insisted Bumblewind.

Star nickered, amused. "I'll be as good as new in a few minutes." Star called up his starfire and sent it racing through his body, healing his wounds from the inside out. The cuts and bites vanished almost instantly. He blasted Morningleaf's swollen leg, restoring it, and also Bumblewind's torn and bruised feathers.

"Thanks, Star!" said Bumblewind, inspecting his wings.

"I'm hungry," complained Dewberry, munching on snow.

Since his birthday, Star didn't feel hunger or thirst like he used to. The starfire supplied energy, renewed him, and fed his muscles. If the elders were correct about his power, he was immortal. He wouldn't age or die. He could be killed only if his body was destroyed beyond his ability to repair it, but otherwise he would live forever. Star avoided thinking about that. His friends were not immortal, and they felt hunger and grew weary, and so he let them rest.

But to find food in this harsh environment, the four of them had to scrape at the snow with their hooves until they found a layer of green lichen. They grazed on the tasteless moss until the last rays of the sun disappeared and the pale glow of the moon cast the only light.

"What was Snow Herd's problem today?" asked Dewberry as she and the others dug into the snow to sleep. "Don't they want to live?"

Morningleaf grimaced. "That was fear."

"Fear of what? Survival?" Dewberry folded her wings around her body.

"That was stupidity," said Bumblewind.

Dewberry nodded. "They deserve to die."

Bumblewind nickered, "For once I agree with you."

Dewberry snorted. "For once! You always agree with me."

"I do not," he whinnied.

"Do too."

Star watched over his friends as they bickered with each other before falling asleep. *What good was his power if the pegasi of Anok wouldn't accept it?* Feeling useless, he focused on what he could do: protect his friends on this cold night and attempt to sharpen his hooves. He found a flat rock and imitated the motions of the warriors. He'd watched them do it a hundred times, but after many long minutes of rubbing his hooves on the rock, they were smoother, not sharper. He would have to learn the secret when he returned to River Herd.

The sky was clear, and he could see his breath blowing from his nostrils and rising toward the stars. The utter silence of the north amplified the smaller noises: the sharp chortles from the animals, the snapping of twigs, and the sudden dumping of snow off overburdened branches. Star's ears flicked as he listened to the sounds and kept watch.

In the morning, Star and his group flew several more hours until they spotted River Herd resting at the base of the Hoofbeat Mountains in the northernmost lands of Anok. Their hides were dusted with fresh white powder, and their coats had thickened in just the few days since they'd arrived. Star landed, and the steeds greeted him with joy. In this foreign, icy land Star relaxed, for with River Herd he was home.

8

CAPTURE

AS RIVER HERD SCROUNGED FOR FOOD IN THE ICE
Lands, Mountain Herd faced starvation. They had over-
grown their territory, and the extra steeds Rockwing had
brought into the herd after the battle in Sky Meadow had
made matters worse.

Since Star received his power, Mountain Herd was on
edge, wondering what his next move would be. Surely the
black foal would not be content leading a tiny homeless
herd. Rockwing was sure Star would reclaim Sun Herd's
territory, or worse, all of Anok. The worried over-stallion
increased his patrols of the land and sky and waited,
working on a plan to gain control of the black foal so he
could take Sun Herd's land and feed Mountain Herd.

Presently, Rockwing's grandson, Frostfire, was standing by Circle Lake thinking and preening his feathers, watching for intruders. It was late winter in the eastern mountains of his territory, and the low sun sparkled on the fresh snow, turning the top layer to slush. The pine needles dripped melted ice that would freeze again during the night, and the rocky creek was frozen dry.

Frostfire startled when a sudden fluttering of feathers in the nearby woods caught his attention. He narrowed his eyes and saw a pegasus watching him from the trees. Frostfire flexed his wings while his mind raced. He'd left his platoon grazing in the lower valley after their ambush drills. Now here he was, alone and possibly being ambushed himself.

Frostfire swiveled his ears, detecting the shifting of many hooves. The pegasus in the forest was not alone. Frostfire was sure the group of steeds had already spotted him. Circle Lake was located in an area void of trees, so he was standing in the open with no protection. He huffed in frustration. He knew better than to leave himself exposed like this. With that thought, Frostfire made up his mind to confront the intruders rather than seek help and admit he'd been caught with his wings down.

"You there!" he whinnied. "Show yourself." Frostfire

kicked off and flew toward the woods. As he approached the band of pegasi, they retreated. He quickly realized they were hiding from him, not stalking him. Feeling bold, he landed and arched his neck. "I said, show yourself." His deep voice brimmed with the confidence of his birth father, Iceriver, and the ferocity of his mother, Petalcloud.

Frostfire peered through the branches. A bay stallion with gray feathers emerged with his head bowed. Frostfire was shocked to recognize the under-stallion. He wasn't an intruder; he was Mountain Herd's flight school instructor, Hedgewind. Hedgewind's yearling students stood trembling behind him. Frostfire's young aunt, Shadepebble, was one of the students, but he didn't see her. "Explain yourself," he commanded Hedgewind.

The bay stallion's lip quivered, and tears formed in his eyes.

Frostfire swallowed his disgust. "Answer me or I'll kill you right here."

Hedgewind's words came out in a whisper. "We were raided by Snow Herd stallions."

Frostfire flared his wings. "What? Where?"

"Over the mountains in the western Vein, near the old Sun Herd lands."

"You left our territory?" Frostfire flattened his ears.

More and more, steeds were sneaking off to graze in the Vein where there was still long grass.

Hedgewind stammered. "Rockwing gave his permission."

"Then why are you hiding here by Circle Lake?"

Hedgewind glanced at the clouds floating in the blue sky above them, trying to gather his words.

"Look at me when you speak," ordered Frostfire.

Hedgewind met Frostfire's eyes, and the words tumbled out of his mouth. "There were seven of them. They took Shadepebble."

Frostfire choked on the spittle that had collected in the back of his throat. Snow Herd stallions had stolen Rockwing's filly! It was unthinkable. "When!" he demanded in a roar.

"This morning."

Frostfire whirled and walloped the instructor with his back hooves. Hedgewind ducked, but Frostfire's blow didn't miss. The bay under-stallion sailed backward, tumbled over his wings, and then crashed into the snow. The flight school yearlings galloped toward the clouds, their eyes round and wild. "Come down," Frostfire snapped at them. They landed and waited, shivering with fear.

Hedgewind coughed blood, splattering the snow in red

droplets. It was high noon. Frostfire guessed the Snow Herd stallions were many hours away with their prize by now.

"I don't think they know who she is," sputtered Hedgewind. "They just took her because she . . . she couldn't keep up with us."

Frostfire exhaled, furious. Shadepebble had been born a dud with mismatched wings. Unable to fly the first five moons of her life, she exercised her muscles each day until she could lift off over the grass. After many more days of practice, she flew to the lowest clouds and back, and then Rockwing had allowed her to attend flight school. Today was only her second lesson. "You didn't go after her?" asked Frostfire.

"No, sir. I was protecting the others."

"Protecting them, or yourself?" Frostfire advanced on the quivering stallion, ears pinned, teeth flashing. "You abandoned Shadepebble and hid like a coward. Do you think you will get away with this?"

"I—I made a mistake," said Hedgewind, humble and trembling.

Frostfire felt nothing but disgust for the old warrior. Hedgewind had lost his taste for battle years ago and had been reassigned to teach flight school. Why Rockwing let him take a flock of yearlings to the Vein alone was beyond Frostfire, but he knew Rockwing would place all the blame on Hedgewind.

Frostfire kicked off. "All of you—follow me." The yearlings and their instructor followed him back to Canyon Meadow, where Frostfire knew Rockwing would not be pleased to hear the news that his last remaining filly had been stolen.

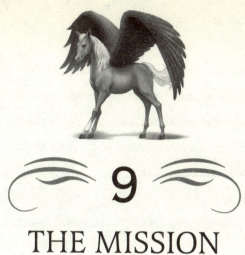

9

THE MISSION

FROSTFIRE FOUND HIS GRANDSIRE, ROCKWING, standing on the outcropping of rock where he'd attempted to execute Star just over a moon ago. The over-stallion was dozing in the sun.

Frostfire settled the yearlings in the valley, and then he and Hedgewind landed next to Rockwing, waking him.

"Speak," said the heavily spotted silver over-stallion.

Frostfire swallowed, hesitating. He knew his words would shatter his grandsire. "I have bad news," Frostfire said. "Shadepebble's been captured by Snow Herd. It happened during flight school."

Rockwing turned his head, slow like a hunting cat, and gazed intensely at Hedgewind. The instructor stood behind Frostfire, quivering and shedding feathers in fear of Rockwing's silence. Then, without a word, Rockwing trumpeted for his personal warriors, and the sound ripped through Frostfire's brain, making his head hurt. Immediately, twelve warriors jetted from the clouds and landed on the rock.

"Seize him," Rockwing ordered, nodding toward Hedgewind.

"No!" Hedgewind neighed as the stallions clutched his wings in their powerful jaws and swiftly dragged him out of sight.

Frostfire exhaled and refolded his ruffled violet-tipped feathers.

Birchcloud, the lead mare of Mountain Herd, dropped from the sky and landed next to them, out of breath. "What has Hedgewind done?" she asked, her voice cracking. She must have heard Rockwing's urgent call for his warriors. Her eyes scanned each of the flight school yearlings, who stood trembling in the grass. "Where's Shadepebble?"

Rockwing stared into the distance, his eyes unfocused, and said nothing. Frostfire answered, "She was kidnapped this morning in the Vein by Snow Herd stallions."

Birchcloud rocked back on her haunches, stunned. Snow Herd had both of her fillies now, one by choice and one by force. "It must be a mistake," she said. "Surely Pet-alcloud will return Shadepebble to me?"

Rockwing snorted, the only sign he was listening. Frostfire knew the over-stallion was already plotting how to get his filly back.

Frostfire nodded to Birchcloud, feeling her fright and sadness. The lead mare had raised him like her own colt and had always been kind to him. "Hedgewind also believes it was a mistake," he said, trying to reassure Birchcloud. "They weren't targeting Shadepebble, just stealing year-lings. But Shadepebble was the easiest to catch."

Birchcloud gasped, her tears falling freely.

Frostfire's feathers twitched. He was anxious to seek revenge on Snow Herd for his stolen aunt. "But you know Petalcloud won't send her back. She cut all her ties with Mountain Herd when she left. She's our enemy."

Birchcloud sagged. "I know, and Twistwing isn't stu-pid. Once he realizes who he's kidnapped, he'll understand the consequences." She closed her eyes. "Returning Shade-pebble would admit error, so he won't do that. Killing her would be his own death sentence, and keeping her will begin a war—he's backed himself against a tree, unless war is what he wants." Birchcloud opened her eyes and moaned with despair. "Did Hedgewind fight for her?"

"No," sneered Frostfire, lashing his tail. "He hid with the students and let them get away with her."

Birchcloud glared at Rockwing, her green feathers standing on end. "I *told* you one instructor is not enough to protect—"

"Hush!" Rockwing neighed, raising his wing. Frostfire knew the two leaders argued often about flight school. Birchcloud had never understood why one instructor took so many yearlings out flying by himself. In light of Shadepebble's capture, her concerns now made terrifying sense.

Rockwing's eyes refocused on Frostfire. "What's done is done. She's gone, and Hedgewind will be punished." He grimaced. "And you're correct about Petalcloud. She'll kill her sister before she'll return her. We don't have much time to get Shadepebble back."

Frostfire pricked his ears. Rockwing had taken the mightiest warriors after conquering Sun Herd. His army was stronger than ever. They could attack in force and rescue Shadepebble. "I'll gather my division of the army," said Frostfire, his pulse thumping at the thought. "I'll have her back in three days, maybe five."

"No, that won't do." Rockwing tossed his mane, his eyes hard and black. "A messenger mare arrived last night and is already on her way to Desert Herd. She said that plague has struck Snow Herd. They call it Blue Tongue, and it's why they're stealing yearlings in the first place. They're trying to replenish the herd. I can't risk exposing your division. We need to send a smaller group."

"A plague?" Birchcloud's wings dropped to her sides, and she stared up at the sky. "Please protect Shadepebble," she whinnied to the Ancestors, her voice rasping. "Leave me one foal."

Rockwing waited for her to calm down, and then he said, "Please leave us to talk, Birchcloud, and don't wail. You know I'll get her back."

Frostfire saw her body relax, but her eyes sharpen as she stared at her mate. "Don't return without her," she said.

Rockwing huffed and pointed at Frostfire. "I'm not going. He is."

Birchcloud turned to him, and her eyes softened. She'd raised Frostfire from a weanling. "May the Ancestors be with you." Birchcloud flew away without looking back.

"When do I leave?" asked Frostfire, looking at Rockwing.

"You'll select a team and leave in the morning. Get in and get out. Avoid the sick pegasi, and that shouldn't be too hard. Twistwing will keep Shadepebble guarded by herself, to keep her healthy."

Frostfire didn't like the idea of leading a small team into Snow Herd's territory, but he understood why it had to be so.

Rockwing drew closer to Frostfire and lowered his voice. "This is only half of your mission."

Frostfire's heart trilled, and he leaned close to Rockwing, eager to hear the other half.

"I was going to send you this summer," said Rockwing, "but now is the perfect opportunity. You're going to kidnap that blue-winged filly Morningleaf from River Herd."

Frostfire gaped. "The one Star brought back to life?"

"Yes. You're going to hide her from him."

"Why?" asked Frostfire.

"For land!" said Rockwing, his chest swelling. "I'm going to take Sun Herd's territory before Star decides to claim it."

Frostfire nodded. It seemed all of Anok was on hold, waiting for the black foal to make a move. It was difficult for a pegasus, let alone a warrior pegasus, to believe Star would remain content without a territory.

A gust of wind ruffled Rockwing's mane. "I have the most powerful army in Anok, but the black foal, by himself, can destroy us all. I don't think he'll stand back and let me take his birth land and the territory of his mother's grave when he has the power to stop me." Rock-wing glowered at Frostfire, shaking his head. "No. This black foal hasn't even begun to use his starfire. I know the legends of Nightwing. I know what black foals are capable of. Star's herd is homeless; he's going to have to make a move for territory, and soon. But I also know his greatest weakness—and it's that pesky filly."

Frostfire agreed, but stealing Morningleaf meant tak-ing a huge risk. Still, Frostfire often dreamed of the lush, green meadows Mountain Herd needed so desperately. While most mares in Anok birthed only several foals in their lifetime, Mountain Herd mares birthed a foal each year. It was a matter of extreme pride for the mares, and it was a custom that made Birchcloud's failures that much more unbearable, but Frostfire saw other effects of the tradition. The Mountain Herd steeds were bursting to the very edges of their territory. They ravaged their grass-lands, consumed thousands of birds' eggs, and were often forced to eat weeds.

This season's foals were thin, and they would make weak warriors in the future. Rockwing had to expand their land or starve, and Sun Herd's territory was perfect. It was currently empty, and it bordered Mountain Herd's western end. The rest of the lands surrounding Mountain

Herd were either inhospitable or occupied by enemy herds.

But did they have to fight for it? wondered Frostfire. "Sir, we don't know for sure that Star will take the Sun Herd lands back."

Rockwing's eyes glittered with malice. "Trust me, when he grows into his stallion blood, he'll want his homeland back. And as long as we control Morningleaf, we can control him."

Frostfire wasn't sure it would be that simple.

Rockwing continued. "Shadepebble's capture makes now the perfect time to leave. No herd will question a search party on the hunt for my filly. You will have an excuse to travel freely through Anok."

Frostfire nodded. "That makes sense."

Rockwing arched his neck, pleased. "My scouts tell me River Herd has traveled north to the Ice Lands. Choose six battle stallions and two sky herders to help you. You leave at dawn."

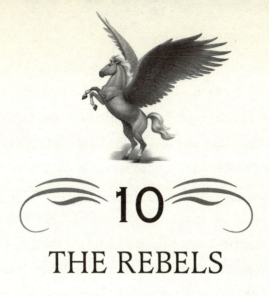

10

THE REBELS

AT DAWN, FROSTFIRE AND HIS TEAM FLEW OUT of Canyon Meadow on their mission. Frostfire had chosen six stallions he trusted, ones he'd trained with in Rockwing's army. Rounding out their group were the two agile mares trained as sky herders: Larksong and Darkleaf. He'd chosen them for their small sizes and fierce natures.

Frostfire knew the odds were high they would never return to Mountain Herd. He had seen the black foal up close the night Star received his power, and Frostfire was not fooled by the colt's peaceful nature. Beneath that unflinching gentleness was a deep-burning fire. He'd seen the colt stuff it down when he chose not to execute Rockwing that night.

Others in Mountain Herd believed the black foal was good, and Frostfire was not blind to the secret gatherings that occurred late at night. The steeds who wanted to follow Star pretended to graze while plotting their escape. When they did, Rockwing hunted them down and executed them for treason. These rebels hoped Star was the healer, but Frostfire doubted it. And stealing Morningleaf might be just the thing that sends the black foal over the edge and in the wrong direction.

The shiny-feathered buckskin mare named Larksong flew at the head of the V formation. Frostfire and one of his stallions each took an end.

As they traveled, Frostfire watched miles of snow-flecked pine trees and smaller areas of aspen trees pass beneath his hooves. The visible terrain was heavily trampled from grazing, and it seemed every bit of edible vegetation had been consumed. The only good thing about this mission was that food would be more plentiful once they left their territory, at least until they reached the Ice Lands.

Frostfire hadn't explained the details of their extra mission to his team yet. If he'd told them back home, he risked someone overhearing or one of his team members confiding in another steed. Kidnapping Morningleaf was too important and too exciting for most pegasi to keep a secret.

But after three days of flying by day and resting at night, Frostfire decided to inform them. They landed in a clump of fir trees near a narrow creek, where they would be shaded from the afternoon sun. Frostfire waited for his special team to drink. He flared his nostrils for the scent of predators but detected nothing unusual. Finally they sensed he was waiting for them, and they gathered to listen.

"It's time I explained our mission," Frostfire began. "I want you to know I chose each of you because I trust you and your abilities."

"You said we were rescuing Shadepebble," said the sky herder Larksong, her black eyes suspicious.

"We are, but that's not all." Frostfire looked at each one of his steeds. "We're also going to kidnap a River Herd filly named Morningleaf."

Each team member made an incredible effort not to react, except the youngest of the warriors. "Who's Morningleaf?" he asked.

The others ignored him, each lost in thought. Frostfire understood. The consequences of this mission were unpredictable.

Darkleaf, the other sky-herding mare, answered the stallion's question in a hushed tone. "Morningleaf is Star's best friend, the filly he brought back to life."

"Ohh," he said in a long exhale.

"For what purpose are we taking her?" asked Larksong. She peered intently at Frostfire, her delicate muzzle blowing plumes of steam in the cold.

Frostfire balked at the forwardness of her question—he was her captain after all, but he also believed he owed his team an explanation. To target a specific steed for a kidnapping was not unheard of, but this one was Star's friend—his best friend. "Rockwing plans to takeover Sun Herd's territory. Stealing Morningleaf will ensure the black foal doesn't stop us."

One of the stallions grunted. "Stop us? He'll *kill* us."

Darkleaf nodded. "He's not going to like us taking her."

"Exactly," said Larksong, pinning her ears. "But we have to do it. Rockwing is correct; Mountain Herd won't survive another season in our small territory, and the Sun Herd lands are sitting empty, for now. We'll die if we don't claim them."

Frostfire relaxed. Larksong's support reassured the stallions, but Darkleaf did not look convinced. In fact, she was backing away from them.

"What's wrong with you?" snapped Frostfire.

Her eyes were round and wild. "I can't be part of this," she whinnied.

Frostfire stepped toward her, and she hunched,

flattening her ears. "It's too late to turn back," he neighed at her.

She trembled and said nothing.

Frostfire swished his tail, irritated. "Rockwing will end you if you abandon this mission."

Darkleaf's coiled muscles sprang, and she galloped into the sky.

"No!" Frostfire whinnied. "After her!" His team kicked off and chased Darkleaf over the tops of the trees. Frostfire gained on her easily and knocked her out of the fog with a swift, hard kick. She toppled through the branches and landed on a large boulder, squealing when her leg twisted on impact. Frostfire and his team landed next to her. "Have you gone mad?" he asked, stepping on her with one hoof so she couldn't rise.

The mare was breathing hard, and Frostfire could see the whites of her eyes. "I won't kidnap Morningleaf," she whinnied, and then she bowed her head. "I believe in Star."

"What? You're a rebel?" How had Frostfire made such a mistake? He racked his brain, but he didn't remember seeing her at any of the so-called secret gatherings. "Well, why didn't you follow him when you had the chance?"

"I was afraid to leave Rockwing," she said. "But I'm not afraid anymore."

"You should be." Frostfire stomped on her wing, breaking it. Her body quivered in pain, and sweat rolled down her hide. She gritted her teeth to keep from screaming.

Frostfire whipped around and faced his team. "Does anyone else here have a problem with kidnapping Morning-leaf?" His eyes flamed with anger. "Tell me now."

Larksong folded her wings neatly on her back. "Quite the opposite," she said calmly. "I'm looking forward to it." The rest of his team nodded their agreement.

"Return home," he said to Darkleaf. With her broken wing and injured leg, he knew she would never make it. They'd flown over dozens of wolf tracks on their way here, and her fresh blood would call the packs to her. And if the wolves failed to come, the bears wouldn't.

"That's a death sentence," whispered Larksong, but Frostfire ignored her.

They all watched Darkleaf limp away, broken winged but with her head held high. Frostfire considered the growing number of rebels in Mountain Herd and wondered if Star's influence on the pegasi of Anok wasn't perhaps more powerful than his starfire.

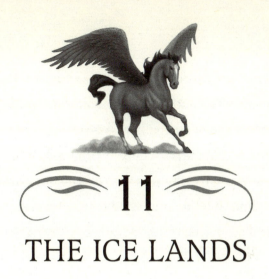

11

THE ICE LANDS

SEVERAL DAYS HAD PASSED SINCE STAR AND HIS
friends returned to River Herd and gave the news that
Twistwing had refused his healing power. "It doesn't
surprise me," Thundersky had said, folding his crimson
wings.

"What about Petalcloud?" asked Silverlake. "Didn't
she argue for the sake of her herd and the unborn foals?"

"She was even less interested than Twistwing," said
Dewberry, and Silverlake had huffed in anger.

Now Star, Bumblewind, and Dewberry were helping
the River Herd steeds dig for roots in the frozen ground.
Echofrost was practicing drills with Hazelwind. She
hadn't spoken to Star since he'd healed Brackentail. Star

was crushed, but Morningleaf insisted he leave Echofrost alone, for now. The cause of the rift—Brackentail—stood by himself, closely watched by his guards.

"How are the mares doing?" Star asked Sweetroot. "The ones I healed?" She was nearby and busy uncovering a special plant she thought could be used for healing.

She looked up, beaming at him. "They're doing well, and their unborn foals are kicking." Sweetroot had quarantined the mares several miles away. Three stallions guarded them at a safe distance. "Their quarantine is over tomorrow."

Bumblewind glanced around him. "Has anyone else showed signs of the plague?" he asked her.

"So far, no."

Dewberry nudged him. "Your tongue looks a little blue."

"What?" Bumblewind splayed his wings. "It does?"

Star rolled his eyes. "Bumblewind, she's just teasing you again."

Star heard the sudden fluttering of feathers and looked up to see Morningleaf flying stiffly across the tundra. He glanced at the sky and noticed that while they'd been digging for roots, a storm had amassed over the Hoofbeat Mountains. Snow drifted from the darkened, large clouds, and a bitter wind blew it sideways.

Morningleaf landed beside them. "I can't feel my muzzle," she complained. Her aqua feathers were dusted with frost, and her eyes had watered during her flight, causing frozen rivulets of tears down her cheeks. She blinked snowflakes off her eyelashes. "I've been looking for you all. This storm is moving fast." She pointed her wing toward the nearest section of the mountain range. "My father and I found shelter there, to the east. It's an ice cave. It won't hold all of us, but we can fit the new foals and the elders inside. The rest of us can group together under the trees."

Star disliked caves. He'd lived in one with Crabwing when he was a weanling, and Star never wanted to live in another. But it sounded like the best—the only—option for River Herd if they wanted to survive the burgeoning arctic storm. "Let's move," he said.

Star and Morningleaf proceeded to gather the River Herd pegasi. Dewberry set out in search of Silverlake. She'd been appointed as a sentry, and it was her turn to patrol the skies. Bumblewind followed her.

Star was saddened by the desolate appearance of the River Herd steeds. Despair had drifted upon them like snowflakes, soft and light at first but then filling every crevice until all other feelings were buried, trapped by the sheer weight of their gloom. The pegasi huddled in miserable, shivering clumps, warming one another as best they could. Their breath rose like smoke, and their eyes were dull.

Star and Morningleaf trotted through the herd, neighing for the steeds to follow. "Morningleaf found shelter to the east," whinnied Star. The wind increased and whistled across the flat tundra, whipping the fresh snow into flurries that blinded him.

"It's not safe to fly in this," said Morningleaf.

Star paused as the dull thud of hoofbeats reached his ears. Someone was galloping his way, but he couldn't see through the deluge of snowflakes. Then a gray shape emerged, followed by another. It was Silverlake and Dewberry. They slid to a halt, out of breath. "One of my sentries hasn't returned," Silverlake whinnied, her expression anxious. "It's Dawnfir; she's late. I have to find her."

Star trotted to her side. "I'll help you look." Dawnfir had been his mother's best friend and was one of Star's most loyal supporters.

"Me too," offered Dewberry.

Silverlake shook her mane. "I'll take one of you, but not both. This storm is too dangerous."

Dewberry looked at Star. "You go. I don't know Dawn-fir that well."

"Thank you." Star squinted across the valley. The falling snow made it impossible to see far. "I'll tell the others we're going."

"No. I already told Thundersky. Let's go now. This storm is only getting stronger," said Silverlake.

She whirled and flew into the snowstorm, Star following. They quickly landed, though, and scanned the tundra. "Let's not fly," she said. "I'm afraid I'll hit a tree." Silverlake's tousled mane blew over her ears, covering her face. She shook off the hair, but it blew right back. The force of the wind caused the snow to fall at a sharp angle, and the hard flakes bit into Star's muzzle like sand fleas. The sky had grown darker still, and the Ice Lands were shrouded in snow.

"It's a whiteout," whinnied Star. "Dawnfir is storm-bound; she can't see to fly. We'll search by hoof, and I'll try and light our way."

He closed his eyes and conjured the warm starfire in his belly, stoking it with his thoughts and growing it bigger and hotter. When it was tumbling through his body, he drew the light up into his throat. The electric fire sparked across his tongue. He opened his mouth and let the golden starlight beam forth. It cut through the thick falling snow and lit their path.

"I didn't know you could do that," neighed Silverlake.

"Neither did I." Star trotted forward, his hooves glowing gold. He wondered what else he could do that he didn't know about. He and Silverlake each spread their wings to shelter their backs from the wet snowflakes. "Where was Dawnfir scouting?" Star asked, his beam of light flickering as he spoke.

"I sent her and another mare south, to Antler Lake. They got separated in the storm, and only one mare returned." Silverlake dropped her head and sniffed the tundra. "With all this fresh snow covering the ground, we won't see her hoofprints, and I can't smell a thing."

Star whinnied over the wind. "Antler Lake is in an open plain. She probably went looking for shelter when the storm hit." Snowflakes landed on Star's eyelashes, half blinding him.

Star broke into a gallop toward Antler Lake.

"No! Wait!" Silverlake neighed, rearing to project her voice. "I'll sweat if we go faster, and then I'll freeze. Let's just trot."

Star nodded and slowed. The starfire beaming from his open mouth shone as bright as day and projected many winglengths ahead of them, piercing the thick cascade of snowflakes. It wasn't long before they arrived at Antler Lake, which was frozen. "Maybe she went that way," said Star, nodding toward rocky hills that would provide some protection from the wind.

Star and Silverlake trotted toward them, their hooves crunching through the frost and slipping on icy rocks. They searched the sheltered sides of the hills for almost an hour but did not find Dawnfir. Star glanced at his adoptive mother. Her white mane and tail had hardened into strands of ice, her legs quaked, and one eye had frozen shut. "Let's stop and rest," he said to her.

She halted, and her body sagged. Her nose dropped to the snow. She shook violently, and her frosty wings collapsed at her sides. "You keep searching, Star," she said. Her voice was rough like her throat was full of gravel. "I'll wait here."

"No. You'll die." Star sidled close and wrapped his wing around her. "I didn't realize how cold you were. I can help you." Star opened his mouth and swathed her in hot gold starfire that did not burn. Silverlake startled, jerking her head upright.

Star swept the fire over her entire body and watched the ice turn to water as it melted off her. When her body was dry and her feathers downy, Star closed his mouth and they stood in the darkness of the storm.

Silverlake nuzzled him. "Your mother would have been proud of everything you've done for us."

Star huffed, and his breath came out in a cloud of fog. How would his mother have been proud? River Herd was starving and on the verge of freezing to death, and it was his fault. Maybe he should have reclaimed Sun Herd's territory. He shook his head, struggling with his doubts.

Silverlake seemed to read his mind. "We're free, Star. We have nothing to fear."

But that wasn't completely true. Half of River Herd would follow him blindly to their deaths. The other half muttered about their living conditions and lack of direct leadership.

"Anyway, I'm proud of you," nickered the mare. "Let's go this way."

Star trotted behind her, lost in thought. So many pegasi had fought and died so he could live and receive his power. They hoped he would heal the herds, but they never imagined the herds wouldn't want to be healed. They didn't foresee that Star wouldn't know what to do.

And the tug he felt from across the sea grew stronger each time he used his starfire, as though the dark force was tracking him. Perhaps in receiving the starfire, Star had woken the hibernating stallion, Nightwing the Destroyer. And what if the ancient pegasus felt the same connection to Star that Star felt to him? If so, then he could hunt Star down and . . . and then what, Star could only guess.

He shivered and halted.

"What's wrong?" asked Silverlake, looking back.

He dipped his head. "It's time I told you something."

She stopped and folded her wings as he approached. "What is it? I'm listening."

"I think Mossberry was right, that Nightwing flew west to hibernate in the Territory of the Landwalkers."

Silverlake's feathers rattled, and she tightened her wings to stop their shaking. Her expression was dazed, as though he'd struck her. "Why are you talking about Nightwing?"

"Because I believe he's awake."

Silverlake gasped. "Why do you think this?"

"I can feel him," admitted Star. "I think we're connected by the starfire."

"What does he want?" She flipped her mane against the wind. "Why would he wake up now?"

"I don't know. It's just . . . the feeling I have is getting stronger, especially when I use my power. It's like he tracks me through it, and I guess I can track him too, because I know he's far away, in the land across the Great Sea. I think his starfire awakened him when I received mine, and now he's coming out of hibernation."

Silverlake drew her wings in tighter. "Is he coming back to Anok?"

Star shrugged. "I don't know."

"You must tell me if anything changes."

She held his gaze for a long time, and Star nodded, feeling terrible. Had he survived his execution and received his power just to awaken the Destroyer? Silverlake seemed to be thinking the same thing, but he couldn't be sure.

Star switched his thoughts back to the missing sentry. "Come on; let's keep looking for Dawnfir."

12

WHITEOUT

STAR AND SILVERLAKE TROTTED THROUGH A
thin forest, the snow crunching beneath their hooves.
"If we . . . don't find Dawnfir . . . soon, we'll . . . have to
head back," Silverlake said, her teeth chattering between
words.

Star saw that her entire face was again dusted in snow
that had turned to ice, but her eyes were bright and determined. Star knew she wouldn't stop looking for the mare,
even though it was clear Silverlake was freezing to death.
He projected his starfire onto her and warmed her again.
"You have to tell me when you're cold, before it gets so bad."

She nodded, and then her ears pricked forward and her
eyes widened. Star listened as a crashing sound pierced

the muffled silence around them, followed by the terrified squeal of a mare. "It's Dawnfir," Silverlake said, and then she whinnied for the mare. "Over here!"

The thumping of hooves and the cracking of branches grew closer. Star lifted his head and beamed light straight into the sky to guide the mare's path toward them. Dawnfir burst out of the shadows, careening jaggedly, her wings tucked tight and sweaty froth covering her chest. Her eyes were white rimmed and her ears flat. "Run!" she squealed.

Star and Silverlake reacted immediately and stampeded with Dawnfir. Star's heart pounded, and his blood whooshed between his ears, wiping out all other sounds. He was faster than the mares, but he ran behind them to protect them—but from what he had no idea.

They galloped madly, leaping over boulders, their heavy hooves breaking branches and slipping over frozen creeks. The last time Star had run—in a confused, panic-stricken terror like this—was during the fire that had killed Mossberry. Sharp branches sliced his chest, and hidden boulders smacked his shins.

The three of them raced out of the forest and skidded to a halt on the open, snowy plain. They were exposed, with nowhere to hide. They could lift off, but they would be flying blind and into a blizzard.

Dawnfir looked back the way they had come, panting. They were each sweating, still hot from running. A sharp growl suddenly exploded from the forest, causing Silverlake to rear, but she held her ground. "What is that? What are we running from?" she asked Dawnfir.

"Bear!" Dawnfir neighed, catching her breath. "But not like any bear you've ever seen." She shook her coat like she was trying to rid herself of the memory.

"Where is it?" asked Silverlake.

Dawnfir glanced around her. "I don't know. I just ran."

"And the bear chased you?" Star asked, peering toward the woods, but he couldn't see a thing. The sky, the land, and the heavy falling snow—it was all a blinding white color.

Dawnfir's sides heaved, and her breath came in short bursts. "I think so. It's been stalking me, actually—like it's smart, like it can think." A shiver ran from her ears down to her tail. She met Star's eyes. "You won't see it; it's invisible. It's not like the black bears that live in our mountains."

Silverlake folded her wings and stepped closer to Dawnfir, peering deep into her eyes. "An invisible bear? I think it's getting dark, and your imagination has flown away with you, Dawnfir."

Dawnfir lifted her chin. "No. It's real, and it's smart."

"Not as smart as us," said Silverlake, ending the discussion.

"Are you hurt?" Star asked, scanning Dawnfir's body for injuries.

"No." She sucked in the cold air and coughed.

Silverlake sighed. "Good, we're together, and we've had enough folly for the day. Let's get back to River Herd."

Suddenly, Dawnfir screamed, and Star gasped as her body was lifted off the ground and thrown across the icy snow. "Dawnfir?" he whinnied. He reared, ready to strike, but saw only whiteness around him. Silverlake skittered sideways, and Star splayed his wings, circling, hunting for the creature that had tossed Dawnfir. It roared, a guttural echo that ended in a high-pitched wail. Star's gut lightened. *Where was it?*

Dawnfir struggled to stand, but two of her legs would not hold her weight. She tried to fly, but her wings only fluttered wildly. Star galloped toward her. The padding of massive paws followed him, gaining speed. The creature growled, a short, chopped sound. Star ran faster. He reached Dawnfir and skidded around her, snatching her tail and tugging on it to help her stand. Her mouth gaped open, and her pupils shrank. "It's right there!" she neighed.

Star whirled and almost didn't see the bear rearing in front of him. It blended perfectly into the white landscape, except for its black nose and eyes. The beast was gigantic, easily four times the size of a black bear. It opened its mouth and roared at Star, the deep rumble of its voice shaking Star's feathers and its hot breath blowing back his forelock.

Star froze, too astonished to move.

The bear swiped at him, and its giant paw connected with Star's shoulder. Star somersaulted and crashed into a snowbank, his right leg stinging as it twisted under him.

The bear dropped to all fours and charged Dawnfir.

"No!" Star whinnied, and exploded out of the snowbank, hopping on three legs and skidding into the bear's path.

Silverlake swooped out of the sky and kicked the beast's head.

It charged past Star, spinning him out of the way. Blood dripped from Star's shoulder, and he stared at the wound. The bear had bitten him!

Silverlake landed next to Star. They galloped forward, but the bear charged them, so they soared above it and resumed kicking at its head with their powerful hooves. The bear ignored them, pawing at Dawnfir and drawing blood. The downed mare rolled onto her back and clubbed the huge beast with all four hooves.

Furious, the bear snatched Dawnfir's blue and white feathers in its claws and dragged her toward its snarling mouth. Anger flushed away the last of Star's confusion, and the starfire flamed inside him, curling through his bones and shooting through his body. He twisted from the sheer intensity of it and almost fell out of the sky.

On the ground, Dawnfir squealed in pain as the bear tugged hard on her wing, shredding the feathers, and then it dived onto her throat.

Star inhaled, expanding his chest with starfire. Silverlake screamed at him, her eyes full of tears, and her words echoed through his brain.

"Kill him, Star!"

13

DESTINY

STAR'S WHOLE BODY VIBRATED WITH WRATH, and his hooves changed from gold to silver. He roared at the bear that was attacking Dawnfir, and the bear roared right back. Dawnfir met his eyes and shook her head, but Star couldn't stop the rage that engulfed him. He opened his mouth and blasted the bear with the silver fire.

The piercing light shot into the bear and lifted it off the snow. Star's heart clamped down, hardening to the bear's pain, leaving Star feeling cold. Darkness swarmed his thoughts until all he wanted was the bear dead. The creature roared and pawed like it was on fire, and Star narrowed his eyes. He drenched the beast in silver flames—to save Dawnfir. The bear clawed at the air like it hoped to run away, but there was no escape, and Star watched it collapse.

Star closed his mouth. His hide sparkled and his hooves glowed silver. He pranced, full of energy, but his heart was as cold as ice. He turned and saw Silverlake staring at him, shocked, her head low and her ears flat.

Star took a slow breath. "Don't be afraid." Silver sparks snapped and fell from his mouth like shooting stars.

Silverlake skirted around him and rushed to Dawnfir's side, but it was too late. The bear had sliced open Dawnfir's throat and belly. Her eyes were absent of life.

Shock and anger blackened Star's vision. Dawnfir—his mother's best friend—was dead, her body too damaged for him to heal. He faced Silverlake and saw his reflection in her eyes, his threatening posture, his silver glow, and the bear's blood smeared across the white star on his forehead. He saw a killer. His gut uncoiled like a snake, and he screamed in fear—of himself. He leaped into the sky, away from her, away from Dawnfir's body, away from the horror.

Star pumped his wings, flying higher and higher. He couldn't see where he was going, and he didn't care. He just wanted to be alone. He flew straight up into the storm, through layers upon layers of wet gray clouds, their moistness choking his breath, until finally he pierced the highest layer and exploded into a clear sky.

It was dusk and the sun was setting, casting long rays of pale light. The stars were out, already sparkling. Star soared over the thick, murky storm clouds that hid Anok from his view. His thoughts swirled with grief and a new sensation: power.

He glanced behind him and saw Silverlake following, but staying low and out of his way. He ignored her, climbing even higher. The silver starfire raced through him, not letting him alone. It seized him like poison, hurting and killing every good thought he'd ever had.

"Star?" whinnied Silverlake from below. "Are you all right?"

Star knew he needed to get rid of the silver poison in his body. He opened his mouth and blasted a plume of starfire so powerful it tossed him backward. The silver light exploded out of him, racing toward space as he exhaled.

When Star felt drained, he closed his mouth and fell, tumbling ears over hooves toward land. The face of a solid-black pegasi with hollow eyes and a ragged mane formed in the sky above him like a living constellation. Star gaped at the almost transparent image. *Trust your eyes, Star,* Dewberry had instructed him.

Star blinked rapidly and refocused. The creature was real, yet unreal. It was a vision of Nightwing, splashed across the sky but looking right at Star. Nightwing bared his teeth and lunged for Star's throat, like the bear did to Dawnfir. Star dodged the shadowy black stallion and shielded his eyes, falling faster toward the cloud layer.

Silverlake jetted toward him, whinnying, "Fly, Star, fly!"

He hadn't realized he wasn't flapping his wings. He hit the cloud bank and fell through it, scattering the mist like silver smoke. He spread his feathers and flipped over, capturing the current until he was gliding.

The apparition of the black pegasus disappeared. Star coughed up the rest of the silver starfire in short bursts, and soon his glowing hooves dimmed and the last of the sparks popped between his teeth. He soared back up toward Silverlake.

"What happened?" she asked, her voice quaking. "Why did your starfire turn silver—it's always been golden?"

Star coasted, exhausted, not knowing what to say.

"It's the power of the Destroyer, isn't it?" Silverlake's voice trembled, on the edge of panic.

They flew out of the clouds and glided over them,

above the storm. He opened his mouth, and the truth tumbled out. "I am both," he cried. "I am the healer *and* the destroyer."

Silverlake gasped. "So it's not the Hundred Year Star's choice what you are? It's yours?"

"Yes . . . no." His voice broke. "It's a choice, but I'm always both. Each time I use my starfire, I have to choose what I am." He took a deep breath, ready to confess more. "Before, when I healed Brackentail's wing, I almost killed him. I was angry. I'm . . . I'm doing my best to control it."

Silverlake tensed but flew on, thinking. After a while she spoke. "You can't tell anyone else. You'll scare them."

"I know," he said, anguished.

Silverlake sensed Star's doubt and misery. "Now, more than ever, you must believe in yourself," she said firmly.

Star trusted Silverlake because they wanted the same thing: what was best for the herds. He could be honest with her. "I saw Nightwing again, just now. It was another vision. I'm afraid of him."

She grimaced. "Focus on who you are, not who he is."

Star tossed those words through his mind. His mother had said something similar in a dream. But who was he? The truth was, he was two pegasi. He was the yearling who wished he was a regular steed like everyone else. But he was also the black foal of Anok, the immortal healer, and the only one who could save the herds from Nightwing.

How could he be both?

"I don't want this," he admitted.

"I know. Your mother had a plan for her life too, but when you came along you changed everything."

Star hung his head.

"The point is that you were her greatest joy. She accepted you, and she died with no regrets. Stop wishing you were something you're not. You need to accept your destiny like she did."

Star wiped his tears, nodding.

Silverlake looked him in the eye. "You used that silver fire to try and save Dawnfir. You did the right thing with your power."

Star's throat tightened with grief, and he couldn't breathe. He just nodded.

"Let's bring her home," said Silverlake.

They returned to the scene, but Dawnfir was gone. A score of huge paw prints circled the bloody snow where she had died.

"Those prints are from ice tigers," said Star, horrified. He scanned the terrain. "It looks like they dragged her into the forest."

Silverlake shuddered. "Please," she whispered. "Let's go back. I don't want to see tigers feeding on her."

Star nodded, feeling as though he'd just woken from a nightmare. He felt the golden seed of his starfire glowing deep inside, warm and comforting once again. With a sinking feeling, he recalled the hollow-faced stallion he'd seen in the sky. Nightwing was awake; Star was positive of that now. But why had he appeared to Star? What did he want?

Star swooped through a cloud, scattering it and feeling weary. Nightwing was using the power they'd both received from the Hundred Year Star to find him. Star didn't know Nightwing's plans, but he did know that there was one thing an over-stallion would not tolerate above all other things—and that was another over-stallion.

With a jolt Star realized Nightwing wasn't the threat—Star was the threat! He had survived his birth, inherited his power, and now lived among the herds of Anok. He was a challenger to Nightwing's reign—a rival. Though the four-hundred-year-old stallion had tired of his immortality and retreated into hibernation, he now had a grand reason to awaken . . . and to return.

14

DIVIDED

THE SHRILL TRUMPETING OF AN OVER-STALLION
woke Star from sleep. He opened his eyes to bright sunlight, melting ice, and peaceful silence. Confused, he looked around for the noise, which must have carried into the Ice Lands from the depths of his dreams.

Star was with River Herd, and the horrible storm was over. He'd been so lost in his thoughts, he barely remembered flying back to his herd last night. Silverlake had given the news of Dawnfir's death and conducted a short memorial, and then Star had collapsed in the snow, overwhelmed. When sleep claimed him, he was grateful.

Now he stretched and shook the snow off his hide. He looked up—the sky was dusty blue. The fresh snow sparkled in the sun, blinding him. Ptarmigans rummaged for seeds and leaves in the weedy bushes, and the call of a bald eagle echoed across the tundra. Star realized it was the eagle's call, not that of an over-stallion, that he'd heard in his half sleep.

He roused Morningleaf and Bumblewind, and they trotted to the entrance of the ice cave Morningleaf had discovered the day before. Inside, the mothers were huddled together, their hot breath warming the cavern, and the newborns were suckling. Silverlake landed next to Star and his friends. "Is everyone accounted for?" Star asked her.

"Yes," she replied, her eyes swollen from crying over Dawnfir, "but the foals are cold."

Star lurched at the chance to be helpful. "I can warm the cave," he said, "like I warmed you during the storm." He opened his mouth, ready to drench the cavern with heat.

Sweetroot overheard and galloped toward him, waving her wings. "Star, no! You'll melt the ice."

Star arched his neck, feeling silly. "Oh, right." The cave was already dripping water from the pegasi's hot breath, and if he blasted the cave with starfire, it would likely collapse. "Sorry," he said, feeling embarrassed.

The newborns and mothers stared at him like he'd just hatched out of an egg. Sweetroot chuckled. "I see you want to be helpful, Star. I have something you can do. Follow me."

Star nodded and followed the medicine mare to a clever shelter she and her apprentice had dug into the lee of a massive snowbank.

Inside the shelter were four steeds wearing miserable expressions. Their hooves were dark purple from standing so long in the ice. "If you could just warm up their hooves a bit, please," the old mare asked.

Star closed his eyes and focused on the power inside him, grateful to be doing something useful. He teased the starfire gently into his mouth, where it tingled on his tongue, then blew warm light onto the frozen hooves.

"Heat them slowly," cautioned Sweetroot.

After a while the hooves began to thaw, and the steeds grunted with fresh pain. Slowly the hooves turned from purple to white and then to a healthy brown—except for one stallion. One of his hooves had turned black and would not warm. His frostbite was severe.

"That'll be all, thank you," Sweetroot said, excusing Star.

Star balked at her words. He nudged Sweetroot out of the shelter and whispered to her. "I can heal his hoof."

Sweetroot paused, thinking. Finally she said, "Warming a hoof is one thing, healing a dead hoof is another. The stallion must accept his fate."

Star flinched. "But he'll be crippled."

"I know that, but you can't go around healing everyone." Sweetroot placed her wing on Star's back, drawing him closer. "Where will you draw the line? Will you bring all our dead back to life? Cure old age? Fix every problem? Will you rob us of our destinies?"

Star blinked at her in amazement. "Are you . . . angry with me?"

Sweetroot softened. "No. But I'm concerned your willingness to help will upset the balance of life. Star, if you make us immortal, we will lose our concept of time, the consequences of our actions, and the preciousness of life. You must use your power with wisdom, and in moderation. The golden meadow is the place where there is no death, no sickness, and no pain—but not here."

Star nodded. "I hear you," he said. He trotted away from the shelter, avoiding the injured stallion's gaze.

"Where's he going?" whinnied the stallion.

Star overheard Sweetroot murmuring to him, giving him the news that Star could not . . . would not . . . help him.

The stallion's agonized whinny rocketed across the snow. "He healed Brackentail the Betrayer, but he won't heal me!"

Disgruntled murmuring erupted from the steeds who'd heard him, and Star wished he could fly into a cloud bank and hide. His solace was that the stallion could still fly and he had three perfectly good legs to use for landing. Still, he would limp and struggle on the ground for the rest of his life.

Morningleaf noticed Star's dour expression and trotted to his side. "Are you thinking about Dawnfir?"

"Yes, and that stallion's hoof, and Snow Herd's plague. I'm confused. My whole life, I just wanted to survive to my birthday." He looked at his best friend, knowing it had been her goal too. "But I never thought I'd make it. Now that I've survived, I have all this power that isn't easy to understand, and the herds are still afraid of me."

"Yes," agreed Morningleaf, "but they can't hurt you now. You're too powerful."

She nuzzled him, and Star realized the source of her joy—she didn't have to worry about him anymore. She'd accomplished her mission, which was to see him to his first birthday.

Star sniffed her mane, smelling fresh air and snow.

"I'm not afraid of being hurt," he said. "I'm afraid of hurting others. River Herd is starving." But it was more than just that. With Nightwing possibly returning to Anok, all their lives would be in danger. But Star didn't want to alarm Morningleaf or River Herd about that until he understood the visions better. He'd told Silverlake, and that was enough for now.

"I will prove to you that you worry too much," Morningleaf nickered. "Look here." She dropped her head and gently nudged the snow off the soil with her muzzle, revealing fresh green shoots. Star saw that the young plants had pushed out of the frozen ground and were stretching toward the bright, low sun.

"You see?" she said. "Soon we'll have plenty to eat." Morningleaf's expression was triumphant.

Star scanned the landscape. Buds that had been absent before the storm had erupted on several trees. "You're right," he said in wonderment. The Ice Lands were fast and dramatic. The seasons changed in seconds, storms came and went in the blink of an eye, the winter days were short, and the nights were long. It was a fantastic and dangerous place, but not at all suited for pegasi during the winter, or even now, in early spring. The fresh buds were a good sign, but they were too fragile to eat. It would be another moon before River Herd could eat their fill.

As if reading his mind, Hazelwind and a group of pegasi approached, galloping toward him and sliding to halt. Star tensed. Hazelwind did not mince words, and his expression was bitter. "We can't survive here with these newborns."

Star knew Dawnfir had been one of Hazelwind's closest friends, and the young stallion was devastated by her death. It seemed it had pushed him over the edge.

Hazelwind continued. "Nor is it safe here. We need an over-stallion, a lead mare, and an army to defend us . . . and to watch for predators."

"Hazelwind, what are you saying?" Morningleaf asked.

Silverlake and Thundersky heard their son's voice and flew over to listen.

"I'm saying, we need a leader," Hazelwind said, glaring at Star. "And we don't have one."

Star pawed the ground, unsure what to say. Hazelwind was right. The herd was starving; they weren't safe. And something needed to be done.

More pegasi, mostly refugees, gathered behind Hazelwind, and among them was Echofrost. Hazelwind threw up his head and neighed so all could hear him. "This group has asked me to lead them to Sun Herd's old territory. It's empty. No one has claimed it." He swept his eyes over the pegasi. "And Sweetroot has lifted the Blue Tongue quarantine. We aren't carriers, so we won't infect the land. Now is the time to go."

Star was not surprised by Hazelwind's words, and he sighed in frustration. The steeds had followed Star thinking he would give them an easy life, a safe life free of pain or death, but Star had disappointed them.

"You are free to go," said Star, surprising himself by speaking without consulting the council first.

"Wait," neighed Silverlake. "Let's discuss this."

"They've made up their minds, Silverlake. We can't force them to stay." Star folded his wings, feeling more miserable than ever. Morningleaf squeezed next to him, reassuring him with her presence.

Dewberry was furious. "It's safer for everyone if we stay together." All eyes snapped to her, and Silverlake exchanged a desperate look with Thundersky.

"Sentries aren't enough to protect a herd," Hazelwind pointed out, looking somewhat apologetically at his mother, who had organized the sentry patrols.

Star gazed at the young stallion. Hazelwind had his sire's powerful build, his dam's calm intelligence, and his sister's decisive mind. He would make a capable over-stallion someday, and clearly his supporters believed in him.

Star felt the heat radiating off Morningleaf's body next to him. She pinned her ears as she listened to her brother, her fury palpable. Star caught her eye and shook his head, hoping to stop her before she blasted Hazelwind with her anger.

Hazelwind's chest swelled, making him appear larger. "We're leaving with or without your permission," he said to the council members.

Bumblewind shuffled his hooves, looking confused. "Why don't we all go back to Sun Herd's territory together?" He looked at Silverlake. Every member of River Herd had gathered now to hear what was happening.

Star listened but shook his head. "Sun Herd's territory is bordered by our enemies: Snow Herd to the north, Desert Herd to the south, and Mountain Herd to the east. And the ocean is to the west. We cannot settle there. War will be hard to avoid in such tight quarters." He threw a helpless glance at Thundersky.

The old stallion seemed to read Star's mind. "I have another idea," he said. "We have time to travel inland, to the center of Anok, before the next batch of foals is born. Legends claim there are rich grazing pastures there and plenty of fresh water."

A shiver passed through Star suddenly, but it wasn't caused by the cold. He glanced at Silverlake, then the western horizon, sure he felt Nightwing's presence. It was almost as if Nightwing was listening to their plan. But Star didn't think it mattered where they settled. If Nightwing returned, the pegasi wouldn't be safe anywhere, but Star wasn't ready to panic his herd with this news. Not until he had a plan of his own.

"How do you know of this place?" Dewberry asked.

"Before I was over-stallion of Sun Herd, I was a captain. I flew the Vein like all captains do, but I also explored the east, past Desert Herd. I wanted to see the ancient territory of Lake Herd."

"And did you make it there?" asked Bumblewind.

"No," Thundersky admitted. "It was too far away. But I do believe it exists."

Echofrost interjected. "I've heard the stories about Lake Herd, and they aren't all good. The interior of Anok is dangerous. There are tornadoes, lightning storms, and an overabundance of wolves. Big wolves. No pegasus has traveled there in almost six hundred years. We don't know what it's like now. The Sun Herd lands are perfect."

"Except for being surrounded by our enemies," snapped Dewberry.

Hazelwind flared his wings. "We're going to Sun Herd

territory. You can join us or not, but your Betrayer is not welcome." He glared at Brackentail. "My steeds won't live with him, under guard or not." Echofrost lifted her chin, and Hazelwind stepped nearer to her. Star saw that the two had grown close.

"We won't abandon Brackentail," said Star, regretting that his support of the yearling continued to upset Echofrost. But the council had agreed earlier not to banish their prisoner.

"Then we will part ways with no hard feelings between us," said Hazelwind.

Morningleaf exploded, rearing and stomping her hooves like an over-stallion. Star pranced out of her way, and every glittering eye turned toward her. Morningleaf's words blasted from her mouth, colder and more biting than the arctic storm that had just passed. "Who said following Star would be easy?" She stared down her brother and her best friend, Echofrost, and then swept her eyes over the rest of Hazelwind's followers.

"But we're starving," one of the refugees said. "And I have a filly to nurse." Her tiny pinto foal fluttered next to her.

"Go ahead," snapped Morningleaf. "Take Sun Herd's land, build your army, and prepare for war, because that is what's coming for you."

"Morningleaf!" whinnied Silverlake. "These are our friends."

Morningleaf whirled around, her aqua feathers rattling and her ears flat. "I'm telling the truth. There is another way for us to live. All herds can be one." Morningleaf hiccuped, sniffling back her tears. "I saw it when I died."

The herd mumbled and whispered in surprise.

"What did you see?" asked Sweetroot.

Morningleaf pricked her ears forward. "I saw all the herds living as one, sharing the land, caring for one another, and being friends."

The gathered steeds lashed their tails. A yearling snorted. "Never!"

An elder mare spat on the ground. "Desert Herd stallions killed my mate. I will never make peace with them."

An older dam shuddered. "My filly was stolen by Jungle Herd."

Flamesky, the filly who'd once teased Star for being a dud, stepped forward. "Both my parents are dead because of Mountain Herd."

"But look at us," said Morningleaf. "We're all from different herds, and we've learned to get along. Let's not separate."

Sweetroot patted Morningleaf's back. "What you saw was the golden meadow, Morningleaf. That world doesn't exist here. It's there." She pointed to the sky with her wing.

Morningleaf tensed but said nothing.

Then Echofrost's voice rose above them all. "I was tortured by Mountain Herd steeds."

The pegasi ceased arguing and turned toward Echofrost. Hot tears fell from her eyes and melted the snow. "And it's *his* fault." She pointed her sleek purple wing at Brackentail, then she looked at Star. "I won't live with him another day. I'm going with Hazelwind."

Bumblewind stood in a pile of his own shedding feathers, his entire body quivering with emotion. "You're leaving me, Echofrost?"

"You can come with me," she said to her twin.

Bumblewind glanced at Star and then back at his sister. "No. I'm sorry, Echofrost, but I won't leave Star."

"Neither will I," said Dewberry. Half of River Herd moved behind Star, and the other half gathered behind Echofrost and Hazelwind.

"Well, we won't stay," Echofrost said. She exhaled, and the tension melted out of River Herd as the pegasi accepted the inevitable: River Herd was splitting. The twins trotted to each other and rubbed their muzzles, exchanging breaths.

Bumblewind nickered into Echofrost's mane, "This is terrible."

She shook her head. "We're going to train an army," said Echofrost. "We'll stick to the western border of Sun Herd's territory, by the Great Sea." Echofrost lifted her chin and looked at Morningleaf. "We will rebuild Sun Herd."

Star's gut lurched at her words. *How could they want to return there?* Grasswing and so many others had died in Sun Herd's territory, and the lush, grassy fields of Sky Meadow were still spoiled by their remains.

"Is it true about the Blue Tongue plague?" asked Bumblewind, looking at Sweetroot. "They won't spread it?"

"They won't," said Sweetroot. "The mares Star healed are still healthy, and no one new has gotten ill since we left the infected area and came here. I believe the sickness is gone." Sweetroot caught Hazelwind's eye. "But you must avoid Snow Herd's territory, and the land where we were staying before coming here. The soil might still hold the plague."

Hazelwind nodded and then looked at his sire, Thundersky. "This is good-bye," he said. "We're leaving now."

The steeds of River Herd rushed forward to embrace their departing friends. Silverlake and Thundersky had long words with Hazelwind. But Morningleaf still refused to look at her brother.

Star watched his friends kick off into the clouds. He'd hoped Echofrost would say good-bye to him, but she didn't. Hazelwind and his followers formed one giant V formation, with an older mare in the lead and Hazelwind following behind.

Morningleaf turned to Star. "I thought our troubles were over," she said, "except for the usual, that is."

He nuzzled her, feeling sorry for himself. "If Thundersky had executed me like he wanted, you'd all be living safely in Sun Herd right now, and your family wouldn't be divided."

Morningleaf jolted and threw her head up in the air. "Stop!" she whinnied, her eyes sizzling. Star's ears drooped at her harsh tone. Morningleaf blinked, staring far away. "Your life is not a mistake," she whispered, and then she turned and trotted after her mother.

Star was shocked by her anger, but he knew she was right. He wasn't a mistake. Too many pegasi had died for him to dishonor their memories by second-guessing himself. They'd fought for him to live, and now he had a purpose: to defeat Nightwing, because the truth was, Nightwing had never left Anok, not really. Fear of him had poisoned the herds for four hundred years. Perhaps it was time Nightwing either reigned or was destroyed forever. And the only pegasus capable of destroying him was Star. His heart tightened at the thought.

He was Anok's last hope.

15

CLOSE CALL

BEFORE STAR KILLED THE BEAR, AND EVEN BEFORE he reached the Ice Lands, Frostfire and his team had left Mountain Herd's territory, rooted out the rebel, Darkleaf, and sent her stumbling home with a broken wing and injured leg. That incident was two days ago. Now the team was traveling in the Vein but would soon cross into Snow Herd's territory, where their journey would become much more dangerous.

Frostfire was in no hurry to find Morningleaf. He had not yet come up with a plan to steal the aqua-feathered filly away from Star, but he was looking forward to finding his kidnapped aunt, Shadepebble. He hoped Rockwing was correct and Snow Herd had quarantined her on her own. She'd be guarded, but not by more than one or two pegasi, he guessed, especially if Snow Herd was short of healthy steeds. He didn't think it would be too hard to extract her from their enemies.

Frostfire landed his team near a thin river to drink. "Let's rest a moment while I decide our path," he said to them. The pegasi drank, grazed, and stretched their wings, their movements awakening small hordes of gnats. Larksong watched Frostfire, as she often did, and her smart black eyes made him nervous. He put his back to her so he could think without her staring at him.

The truth was, he was also looking forward to seeing his mother, but he would never admit that to his team. What grown stallion pined for his dam? Frostfire hated himself for his need of her. She'd tricked his father and traded him for her freedom, leaving him with Rockwing, the sire she despised. And she'd lied to him. Frostfire swallowed as his throat tightened, remembering that day.

He was five moons old and had just weaned. To celebrate, his mother told him he would go on a special flight into the clouds with one of her captains. Frostfire's heart had soared at her words—he would fly with a warrior and finally touch the fluffy clouds. He'd been thrilled at the idea and thanked his mother. Petalcloud had nuzzled him, and she'd looked happy too—that's what killed Frostfire. She was happy!

The stallion had escorted Frostfire on his first cloud flight, and it had been magnificent. But after playing in the white mist, the captain led him south and then east until Frostfire became exhausted. "Where are we going?" he'd asked. But the captain ignored him.

When they'd reached the canyons of the Blue Mountains, the captain and Frostfire landed. "Wait here," he said, then flew away, leaving Frostfire alone. Frostfire's chest heaved at the memory of himself hiding in the rocks, bleating like a newborn. He'd been terrified; he couldn't deny it.

Then Rockwing himself had descended from the ridge. Frostfire trembled with fear. Rockwing examined him, making a face when he noticed Frostfire had one blue eye and one brown. The over-stallion said, "At least you're a colt, but if you want to live with me, you'd better toughen up."

"Yes, sir," Frostfire agreed, remembering that this over-stallion was his grandsire, but his mind had been reeling. *I don't want to live with you,* he thought.

"And if I ever see you crying again, I'll kill you."

Frostfire wiped his tears. "Yes, sir."

"Come on then," neighed Rockwing, and he'd flown up

and over several ridges to Canyon Meadow. The next day Mountain Herd migrated to their southern lands, and by the time they arrived, Frostfire could not remember his mother's face. It was a black splotch in his mind, and no matter how hard he tried, his brain would not reveal her features to him.

Shrugging off his memories, Frostfire lashed his tail, striking his flanks and letting the sharp pain distract him. He didn't care about Petalcloud, of course he didn't, but still, he had to see her, to settle his mind.

"So what's the plan?" questioned Larksong.

Frostfire bristled. Sky herders were independent thinkers—they had to be in order to make snap decisions while herding enemy steeds into well-planned traps. But his warriors had been trained to obey orders instantly, and Larksong's incessant questioning grated on his nerves. "Why do you want to know?" he snapped. "Are you afraid of Snow Herd?"

As he'd hoped, Larksong shut her mouth.

Frostfire lifted his wing to get the attention of his team. "We're crossing into Snow Herd's territory today," he announced. "Look for signs of trampled snow, broken ice, and hoofprints. We must spot them before they spot us."

Frostfire's team murmured, excited to take back what

had been stolen from their herd: their over-stallion's filly, Shadepebble. Only Larksong was impatient for a different reason. She wanted to hurry so the team could move on to the more dangerous half of the mission: capturing Morningleaf. And after Rockwing used her to gain control of the lush territory of Star's homeland, Larksong and the team would become legends in Mountain Herd for their bravery.

Frostfire glanced at the buckskin mare, admiring her fearlessness. "This is the plan," he said to them all. "Once we locate Shadepebble, we get in and out. This shouldn't take too much time if we're quick."

Larksong brightened at this news.

"I will take the head wind." Frostfire kicked off, with his team following him. It was evening, but the moon was bright and lit up the sky. Frostfire soared, traveling northwest, and several hours later, they crossed the border into Snow Herd's territory.

"Drop," he neighed, lowering his neck and diving toward land. His team maintained formation and dropped with him. Frostfire flew a winglength above the snow to keep from being spotted.

He decided he liked traveling by night, when fewer sentries were posted. Unlike land horses, pegasi required many consecutive hours of deep sleep. During the day, when the steeds were scattered across their territory, over-stallions kept a vigilant eye on the skies for intruders. They organized patrols and watched the land. But at night the pegasi gathered together and kept a single watch, which was relieved every few hours by fresh pegasi.

"It's so cold," nickered Larksong, her teeth chattering.

Frostfire ignored her and focused on the landscape, looking for the reflective eyes of predators or the glimmering feathers of enemy pegasi.

Just before dawn, Frostfire and his team crested a small hill and halted, hovering in midair. "Would you look at that," huffed a stallion.

Below them, all of Snow Herd slept in a shallow valley.

Frostfire quickly fluttered to the ground, followed by the others, and they flattened themselves into the snow. Frostfire examined the area. The landscape was wide-open to the edge of a small forest, which rimmed the valley. He looked up. A clump of clouds had passed over one-half of the moon, somewhat darkening the sky, but the stars were bright. They were downwind of Snow Herd, which was good for Frostfire's team.

"When the rest of that cloud covers the moon, we'll trot to those trees, where we can hide," whispered Frostfire.

They waited a few moments until the wide cloud traveled in front of the moon. "Go." Frostfire led his steeds through the soft snow, which muffled their hoofbeats. They lowered their wings to shield their quick-moving legs from attracting notice. The small hill blocked the shorter steeds from view.

Frostfire peeked over the ridge and noticed that the Snow Herd steeds were gathered into awkward groups, in various states of quarantine, just as Rockwing had predicted. Frostfire hadn't meant to land so near them, and he feared exposing his team to Blue Tongue. Most plagues affected the very young or the very old, and his team was healthy, so he shook thoughts of illness from his mind.

Frostfire recognized the olive-green feathers of Twistwing, the new over-stallion of Snow Herd. Twistwing dozed while his sentries kept an apathetic watch. Frostfire scanned the herd for Shadepebble and Petalcloud. His belly flipped at the thought of his mother. While he liked to imagine her as ugly, with shallow, beady eyes, he'd heard stories about her exotic beauty his entire life, and he'd soon learn if they were true.

One of his stallions tensed, catching his breath. Frostfire and the others followed his gaze, and there she was, his mother, standing under a beam of moonlight. Frostfire let out a short, hard breath, and agony wrung his heart.

Petalcloud was exquisite, nothing like he'd imagined. The lines of her compact body curved with graceful, powerful precision. Her delicate muzzle widened into a broad, proud nose, and her large eyes angled into soft slants. Her coat, thick from winter, was sleek, unlike the fuzzy Snow Herd steeds, and the color was that of dark smoke. Her silver mane and tail were the same shade as the moon itself. She folded and unfolded her wings, preening her violet feathers.

"That's your dam, right?" asked Larksong in a low nicker.

Frostfire nodded, unable to speak. Her face brought shocking, long-buried memories of his foalhood rushing back to him. *He'd been happy living with her!* His mother had played chase with him and slept with her wing over his back, and she'd nipped the yearlings who'd made fun of his one blue eye.

Frostfire took a deep, ragged breath, understanding finally why his anger had always been buried under a mountain of sadness. Petalcloud *had* loved him, but in the end she'd loved herself more, and when she'd given him away, it was like she'd died. The mother who'd licked his ears and told him stories had been murdered by the mother who'd wanted to rule a herd. He dragged his sharpened hoof through the ice decisively. He wanted nothing to do with the mare she'd become.

As if sensing his presence, Petalcloud suddenly lifted her head and stared in his direction. Frostfire and his team held their breaths, not moving.

Seconds passed, which felt like hours, and Petalcloud tucked her wings and closed her eyes. Frostfire exhaled. She hadn't seen them, but he'd seen her. It was enough. He'd looked into her eyes; and what he'd noticed, besides the beautiful shape of them, was the coldness there, like a lake that had frozen all the way to the bottom.

"Look," whispered Larksong, pointing to a cluster of foreign pegasi. "They've stolen weanlings and yearlings from Desert Herd and Jungle Herd—but I don't see any from Mountain Herd."

Frostfire studied the group of terrified young pegasi. The weanlings' eyes were swollen from crying. The older yearlings rattled their feathers at the guards, looking fierce. They were separated from Snow Herd but not out of sight, and eighteen powerful warriors guarded them.

"What now?" asked Larksong. "Shadepebble isn't here."

Frostfire took a final look at the Snow Herd steeds,

also seeing no sign of his aunt, "We go," he whispered. He led his team to the trees where they were safe for the moment, and they were lucky they hadn't been spotted, because there wasn't much cover in the north. Once the sun rose, their luck would run out.

Frostfire peered east and saw a bright stripe appear on the horizon. "The sun is coming up. We have to get out of here quickly." He pointed at the rising light. "Fly straight into the sunrise. It will hurt your eyes, but it will blind them to us if they look our way. It's now or never."

Frostfire glanced at each one of his teammates. Their pulses raced, and their wings vibrated. They nodded, trusting him. In that second he finally bonded with them. They would live or die together. He faced the yellow dawn. "Fly."

Frostfire erupted from the trees, with his steeds following. They didn't look back as they flew low and fast, skimming the snow with their hooves. Frostfire's breath came quick and hot. He felt his blood rushing through his wings. If the group was spotted, Twistwing would send warriors without hesitation. As sick as Snow Herd was, the stallions appeared healthy enough to fight.

They flew for hours before landing on a rounded hill. It was full morning now. His team gasped for air. Frostfire looked back and saw an empty sky. "We made it."

Larksong shoved her nose into the snow and ate mouthfuls of it, her sides heaving and dripping sweat.

"Let's walk awhile," said Frostfire, "give our wings a rest." He led his group to an icy lake, and beyond it was another forest, so dense the sunlight couldn't penetrate it.

"That's the Trap," said a gray stallion, pointing to the thick woods.

"Yes. The southern end of it," Frostfire replied. "If Rockwing's scouts are correct, Star and his herd are just north of here."

"Was that all of the Snow Herd steeds back there?" asked Larksong.

"I think it was," said Frostfire. "I saw Twistwing and Petalcloud and many stallions but few mares, weanlings, or elders. They wouldn't leave their weakest steeds by themselves, so they must be dead."

"The Blue Tongue plague is wiping them out," Larksong said, looking pleased. "Snow Herd is vulnerable. It would be a good time for Mountain Herd to attack them."

Frostfire nodded. "We should inform Rockwing of their losses. They are worse off than I ever imagined. But where is Shadepebble?"

"Maybe she got the plague and died," said Larksong.

Frostfire bristled at the harshness of Larksong's words because he was fond of Shadepebble. It could be true that she had died, but he didn't think so. Most illnesses incubated first and then killed slowly. Of course this was a plague and not most illnesses.

The image of his mother's cold eyes surfaced. He would not be surprised if Petalcloud had murdered her sister. She could claim Shadepebble had died of the plague, and Rockwing would never know the truth.

But Rockwing could still blame Snow Herd for Shadepebble's death, for exposing her to the illness. He could still start a war with them. So where was she? Frostfire glanced at Larksong, thinking to discuss it with her, but he stopped himself. He didn't want her to know he felt confused.

Shaking his head to clear it, Frostfire spoke to his team. "Two of you will return home. Tell Rockwing about Snow Herd's condition and that his filly is not with them." He didn't wait for volunteers, knowing none of his steeds would want the task of giving Rockwing bad news about his filly. Frostfire picked out the two youngest stallions. "Stay safe and follow the Vein to our territory."

"Yes, sir." The stallions lifted off and flew south.

Frostfire had five steeds left: four warriors and

Larksong. They flew north along the edge of the Trap until dark, then he landed them. "Rockwing's scouts last spotted River Herd traveling to the Ice Lands to avoid the Blue Tongue plague. Hopefully they are still there and haven't moved."

"There's nothing to eat in the Ice Lands," complained a stallion.

"There has to be," argued Larksong. "Animals live there. Big animals," she added.

"He makes a good point though," said Frostfire. "Star's herd could be on the move to avoid starvation. We'll shelter in the woods for the night, but we'll keep watch. Star and Morningleaf could be anywhere."

Frostfire led his mare and stallions to a lake. They chopped at the ice with their hooves and then drank the cold water slowly. He glanced at the snow clouds developing overhead. "After this storm passes, we'll fly to the Ice Lands and begin our search for Morningleaf."

Frostfire kept watch while his team fell asleep in the thick forest that was as dark and foreboding as the black foal himself.

16

ACCEPTANCE

STAR AND HIS HERD MARCHED SOUTHEAST, beginning their journey toward the interior of Anok. The River Herd pegasi were grateful to be on the move, even though no one was sure the lush and windy flatlands truly existed. Anywhere was better than the frozen north.

They traveled by hoof because the newborns weren't ready to fly higher than the trees, the still-pregnant mares were too close to giving birth to fly, and one filly couldn't fly at all—her bright-blue wings were too small to lift her off the ground.

The quarantined mares had rejoined the herd and still showed no signs of the Blue Tongue plague. Their unborn foals grew steadily in their bellies.

Star, Morningleaf, Bumblewind, and Brackentail followed at the rear of the herd, and Silverlake chose their path. Now that Echofrost was gone, Brackentail sought their company more often, in spite of the awkwardness between them. His guards kept near, but since Brackentail hadn't caused any trouble since joining River Herd, they didn't watch him too closely.

Star's herd slowly approached the Hoofbeat Mountains to the east, but Silverlake decided the terrain was too steep and icy to cross by hoof. Since the mountains formed a natural barrier to the interior land, River Herd was forced to travel south, to the end of the massive mountain range. There the herd could turn either east and take a shortcut through the Trap or they could continue south and skirt around the dense and dangerous forest.

Star guessed Silverlake would want to avoid the Trap. The intertwining branches of its trees created an impenetrable ceiling, blocking the sky. It was called the Trap because a pegasi who entered the forest could only escape from it by hoof. And a grounded pegasus was an easy target for bears, wolves, and lions—and those predators were plentiful. On the other hand, the Trap was a shortcut, and traveling through it would trim many days off their journey.

Without warning, Silverlake halted, ears pricked, wings tensed, her every feather standing on end. The River Herd steeds froze behind her, and all eyes scanned the landscape, including Star's. "There," Silverlake whispered.

Star followed the direction of her gaze and saw the lumbering white bear. He gasped and stumbled back, remembering Dawnfir. Star's grief and anger caused the silver fire in his belly to shudder into a biting spark. Star clenched his jaws and resumed walking, trying to ignore the sensations battling inside him.

"She sees us," said Silverlake. The bear's belly was round with unborn cubs. She padded across the sparkling snow, her head swinging from side to side.

Star noticed that the bear was keeping an eye on them, but she picked up her pace and kept moving, not interested in tangling with a herd of pegasi.

"We're safe if we stay together," Silverlake said calmly, eyeing the foals.

The bear continued on her path without threat, and River Herd did the same.

Morningleaf nickered to Star. "Look at my father."

Star's eyes found Thundersky, cantering beside Silverlake with his hooves in a jumble. He fluttered his wings to keep his balance, his expression grouchy. In all his life he'd never traveled this far on land, and they had only just begun.

"Remember when he forbade me to travel by hoof?" whispered Morningleaf.

Star nodded. It was when he was still a dud and his wings dragged on the ground. Just thinking about it caused his shoulder blades to ache. Morningleaf had offered to travel with him, and Thundersky had balked, saying, *"I won't have my filly traveling by hoof like a common horse."* "I remember," Star said.

"Now look at him," she whinnied.

Bumblewind grunted. "Grasswing was the best when it came to traveling on the ground."

Tears sprang to Star's eyes at the thought of Grasswing.

"I'm sorry," said Bumblewind, noticing the heavy pause in Star's breathing.

Star wiped his eyes with his feathers, suddenly realizing why he was sad. With Grasswing and Mossberry dead—and Silverlake confused about his powers—Star had no elders to guide him. "I miss Grasswing," he said simply. Even with his best friends cantering beside him, Star felt alone.

They continued on, trailed by Brackentail, and Star was lulled by the smooth cadence of Morningleaf's hoofbeats. They had a long journey ahead of them. It would be at least a moon before they reached the flatlands in the interior.

That evening they settled near a flowing river. "The snow is melting," said Dewberry, joining them.

The pegasi dug into the tundra with their sharp hooves and feasted on the fragile lichen. The mothers, newborns, and elders lay down in the center of the herd. The rest formed a protective circle around them.

Star watched Brackentail as he pawed the ground, eating listlessly. The herd had become adept at ignoring his presence, and Star remembered how that felt. When a newborn wandered too close to the Betrayer, its dam whinnied a warning, calling her foal away. Star saw that this saddened Brackentail.

Right then Brackentail looked up and caught Star watching him. The two stared at each other for a long time, so long the herd noticed and grew tense. Star huffed, blowing fog from his nose, and then he walked to his old-est enemy and stood in front of him.

Brackentail hunched in Star's shadow but met his eyes. Feelings like lightning raced between them: distrust, anger, fear, and regret. Brackentail pinned his ears, ready for a fight, but Star did not advance. He just stared at

Brackentail, his ears forward, waiting. Brackentail's ears twisted, and his eyes softened. He lowered his head, looking at Star's hooves, and exhaled, surrendering to Star in front of the entire herd.

Star had won the standoff and could drive him off or kill him, but he chose to do neither. He touched muzzles with Brackentail and blew softly into his nostrils, accepting the yearling into River Herd.

"Come with me," Star said to Brackentail, dismissing the guards with a flick of his tail. The big stallions glanced at Thundersky, who nodded, and then they trotted away. Brackentail's breath pumped fast as he followed Star through the herd. Star walked with his head high, and the herd made way for him and Brackentail to pass through. When Star reached his friends, he stopped. "There's untouched lichen here," he said to Brackentail. The four yearlings who'd been foals together all stared, their hearts racing.

And then Morningleaf nuzzled Brackentail, and so did Bumblewind. The big, brown yearling dropped his head and grazed with them, relief and joy tumbling in his eyes. All River Herd relaxed and prepared for evening.

Star glanced at Morningleaf, and she nodded her approval. The four of them, plus Dewberry, grazed together for the rest of the evening.

Later, as everyone slept, Star stayed awake, staring at the beautiful sky. Suddenly he saw a swirl of bright lights appear against the blackness, twisting and floating in a vibrant display. He nudged Morningleaf awake, and she nudged Bumblewind. Steed by steed, the pegasi woke one another. "It's the Ancestors!" neighed Sweetroot. "They're migrating."

All pegasi knew their Ancestors lived in the stars, but few had ever seen them. Their ethereal bodies were invisible to the living, but their bright feathers left streaks of colorful light that could only be seen in the far north.

"Can they see us?" asked Morningleaf.

"I think they're aware of us," nickered Sweetroot.

"Dawnfir is up there," said Silverlake, and her wings relaxed at her sides as she gazed at the incredible colors.

The iridescent lights reflected off Morningleaf's eyes, making them shine. "I was with them," she breathed, "almost." All eyes jolted to her. Morningleaf's death was not something the steeds liked to discuss. How she had died and then come back to life confused them, even though they were grateful Star had healed her.

"Grasswing is there too," Star whispered, "and my mother." His eyes followed the bright colors drifting over his head. There was pale green—Grasswing—and streaks of silver—Lightfeather—and shimmers of magenta— Mossberry. Star lowered his head, and all around him, the pegasi of River Herd followed his lead, bowing their heads to the Ancestors.

"We're not alone," murmured Morningleaf.

"You're right," said Star, returning his gaze to the night sky. His mother and Grasswing had died, but they weren't gone. They lived in the heights and flew through the stars. His heart filled with pleasure. They were on an eternal high flight, past where the blue sky turned black, to where he wanted to fly someday—in space, with the moon as his guide. His mother was there, watching him, swirling above Anok like an evening rainbow, and she was more beautiful than any living thing.

Star gazed beyond the twinkling sky, to the glossy ice and the rugged mountains that stood like sentries in the night. Miles upon miles of glittering white snow surrounded him, and a shallow bubbling creek spoke of the end of winter. Anok and its inhabitants, down to the smallest insect, were magnificent.

Star glared toward the west and folded his wings, resolved in his purpose. He was Nightwing's rival, and he would have to fight him—sooner or later. Star was only a yearling and had never been in battle, or even sharpened his hooves; but he had the power from the Hundred Year Star, and he had a destiny—one his mother believed was good. He would learn to use the silver starfire, even though it robbed his mind of light, and he would protect all of Anok from the destruction that was coming.

Or he would die trying.

17

THE VISIT

LATER THAT NIGHT, AFTER THE LIGHTS OF THE
Ancestors had faded away, Star fell asleep and was soon
sucked into a terrible dream.

*Star cantered through a thick cloud, dispersing it. He
dived toward Anok and then shot upward, seeking the
sun and bucking like a foal. He whinnied, and the sound
boomed across the planet. He felt as big as a mountain.*

*When he reached the highest heights, he coasted on a
jet stream. Below him he saw eight continents and a large
grouping of islands. Anok was only a small part of the
world, and he'd thought the land of the pegasi was so large.*

He wondered where his friends were.

A small white mare was suddenly at his side. "Follow

me," she said, veering off toward the sea. Star flew behind her, soothed by her presence. They glided over the waves for many days, toward the Territory of the Landwalkers. Finally she landed on a beach. It was foggy and cold. Star landed beside her.

"You've grown," she said.

He looked at her face. "Mother?"

She leaned into him. It was Lightfeather! Star buried his nose in her mane. "I miss you."

Her dark eyes were thoughtful, happy, and sad, all at once. "I miss you too," she nickered.

Star's tears fell freely onto the sand, and white flowers sprang between the coarse grains. "I don't know what I'm doing, Mother."

Lightfeather whispered, "Do any of us? We do our best."

"What if that's not good enough?"

"It has to be."

Star nodded, pausing before he said, "Nightwing is coming back. I can feel him."

"I know."

Star stared east, toward Anok. "I'm afraid. Not for myself, but for my friends. For the herds. What if I can't defeat him? What if he's stronger?"

Lightfeather swept her wing over his cheek. "Maybe

you're not stronger, but you're better, Star. Follow your love, not your fear." Lightfeather turned transparent. He could see a dark cave carved in the cliff behind her.

"What do you mean?" he asked.

But before she could answer, Lightfeather's image evaporated, and Star faced the mouth of the cave alone. He heard a rhythmic thudding and realized it was his heart beating. A set of eyes, glowing silver, appeared in the dark maw of the cave, watching him.

"Who's there?" asked Star.

A midnight-black stallion slowly emerged from the dark. He blinked at the vibrant sun and stretched his wings. His coat was covered in dust and rat droppings. Star backed away. The stallion cocked his head, looking surprised to see Star standing on his beach. He recovered quickly, narrowing his eyes. "You survived to your birthday," he said, coughing puffs of smoke.

Every muscle in Star tensed.

The black stallion nickered, as if amused. "You're going to regret that." The words dripped off his lips.

Star shook his mane, the beat of his heart pulsing between his ears.

The stallion dipped his head. "And who is your friend?" Nightwing pranced closer, his eyes bright with interest.

Stunned, Star turned and noticed a pegasus standing next to him, and his heart sank when he recognized her: Morningleaf.

Before he could stop her, she reared, baring her teeth. "I'm Morningleaf!" she snapped.

Star leaped in front of her, but too late to stop Nightwing from scorching her with fire. She exploded, littering the beach with her blue feathers.

"No!" Star screamed, waking up. Sweat rolled down his hide, and he was out of breath.

"What's wrong?"

He turned to find Morningleaf, yawning and stretching her wings. Star watched her blink the sleep out of her eyes. She was curled in a shallow depression she'd carved out of the snow and was bleary-eyed like a foal.

Star shook off the nightmare. He was safe. Morningleaf was safe. "Nothing," he said. "Just a dream." But he knew it was more than that. Nightwing sometimes used dreams to visit Star, and so did Star's mother. He figured they were both trying to tell him something, but visions were confusing.

Star closed his eyes. In the dream, his mother had flown him to the Territory of the Landwalkers, showing him the cave where Nightwing lived. And Lightfeather had confirmed that the Destroyer was returning to Anok. Star could no longer deny the inevitable. The experience had felt so real; Star could still smell the dark stallion's breath. And Nightwing had not been happy to see him.

Star inhaled sharply, realizing that his visit to Nightwing had surprised the stallion, which meant Nightwing hadn't initiated the visit—Lightfeather had! Chills ran down his feathers, standing them on end. Star had shown up at the Destroyer's domain unexpectedly and seen his hiding place. Of course Nightwing would feel threatened by that.

But what about Morningleaf? Had Star brought her with him, or had she tagged along through her own dream? He didn't like that Nightwing had seen her face. Star shuddered. He would speak to Silverlake about the strange visit later.

"Just a dream?" asked Morningleaf, looking doubtful.

He nodded, glad that she appeared to have no memory of it herself. Star thought of Nightwing setting her on fire, and his heart trilled, forcing a rush of blood through his veins.

Morningleaf folded her wings and faced him, sensing his mood. "What are you not telling me, Star?"

He blinked at her, fighting for words. He wanted to

hide her, to surround her with an army—to protect her from what was coming. But how could he tell her that? He sighed. The truth was, he couldn't. She would have none of it.

Morningleaf snorted and returned to preening her feathers. "You know you'll tell me eventually."

Star guessed he probably would. He rotated his ears, picking up the sounds of River Herd wakening. Morningleaf smoothed the aqua feathers that had shifted out of place during the night, looking lazy and content. "I wish we could fly the rest of the way to the interior," she said.

"I agree, but at least cutting through the Trap will shorten our travel time." The council had made the decision to walk through the huge forest instead of around it because of the pregnant mares and newborns.

"I don't care how long it takes us to get there," said Morningleaf. "I just want to fly."

"Me too." Star looked at the River Herd steeds stretching in the snow; at the newborns flitting over the ice, nickering at their reflections; at the elders huddled together to stay warm; and at the fierce mares and stallions who'd sacrificed safety and comfort to be with him. With overwhelming awe, he realized they were his new guardian herd.

These pegasi weren't just following Star, they were protecting him. He knew that, whatever happened, River Herd would be there for him. Bolstered by this knowledge, Star shook off his gloom. He whimsically scooped up a ball of snow with his wing and threw it at Bumblewind, who was just trotting by.

"Hey!" Bumblewind nickered. He scooped up a huge pile of snow and tossed it onto Star and Morningleaf. She squealed and lurched to her hooves. Star joined her, and they chased Bumblewind by air, flying low and scooping up snow between wingbeats. Several mares and stallions joined in, nickering and bombing each other while the dams shielded their faces. Even Brackentail joined in the fun after Morningleaf's well-aimed shot exploded against his chest.

With a focus usually reserved for battle, Dewberry scooped up a clump of hard ice and pitched it at a stallion so forcibly, she knocked him to his knees. Surprised but not offended, the stallion whinnied and charged her, playfully smashing a wingful of wet snow down her neck.

Star landed, his sides heaving and his heart a bit lighter from the game. The sun was brilliant this morning, and more buds had appeared on the trees. Birds chirped deep in the Trap, and he saw that some light rays broke through the heavy ceiling of branches. Maybe their journey through the dark forest would be more pleasant than he'd anticipated.

"You all are starting to sweat," warned Sweetroot. The playing steeds landed, dropped their wingfuls of snow, and fanned their feathers to dry themselves. It was dangerous to be wet for too long in the freezing north.

Silverlake whistled for the herd to move out after breakfast. They traveled companionably now; their tension over Hazelwind leaving had eased as the days passed. Brackentail kept close to Star and Morningleaf, but the big brown yearling didn't speak much to either of them. He kept pace and listened attentively to the steeds around him. His wounds had healed into pink scars that were beginning to grow hair.

The day was blustery, but the sky was blue and the sun was warm, and Star was as content as he could be.

River Herd had exited the Ice Lands, and they were at the southern end of the Hoofbeat Mountains. The Trap was visible, but they hadn't reached it yet. After miles upon miles of open, flat land bordered by stark, steep mountains, the impassive forest faced Star and his herd like an army, daring them to enter. Walking together through the Trap would be impossible; the trees were too close together. They would have to divide into small groups of four or five pegasi.

"Look there!" neighed Iceriver, suddenly alarmed.

Star tensed and followed Iceriver's gaze. In the distance, the head of a struggling horse popped out of an icy pond. The horse was wild eyed and drowning. Star kicked off and flew toward her, followed by his herdmates. Star reached the pond first.

Beneath the water he saw pink feathers. It wasn't a horse; it was a pegasus!

18

RESCUE

STAR HOVERED OVER THE YEARLING FILLY WHO
was drowning in the pond. "Relax," he nickered, attempt-
ing to soothe her panic.

She tried to speak but choked on the water. Her front
hooves thrashed, chopping at the ice. She slipped under,
reemerged, and then slipped under again. Her small body
sank, drifting toward the bottom, and her wings floated
up as she dropped.

Star angled his feathers, flapping his wings so fast
they blurred, and he flipped his body so he was hovering nose down over the water. He thrust his head beneath
the surface, and the shocking coldness burned him like
fire. He seized the root of the filly's left wing in his teeth

and pounded his wings, slowly lifting her up and out of the water. She was struggling and waterlogged, and he couldn't lift her clear. He dragged her out of the water and slid her body onto the solid ice, pulling her across it, and then released her onto the shore.

Sweetroot arrived and took charge of the half-drowned yearling while Star shook the frigid water out of his mane. Sweetroot ordered two steeds to massage her chest and two others to fan her dry. "Roll her over," she said to Star. "I think I saw a wound."

Star pushed her over with his nose and winced when he saw the parallel scratches of a giant animal, like a tiger or a bear.

"She looks like a Mountain Herd filly," said Morningleaf. She cupped her wings over the filly's face and used her hot breath to warm the air between them. "What is she doing alone in the north?"

Iceriver scanned the skies. "She might not be alone."

River Herd huddled together while Sweetroot worked. The gusting wind kept blowing the medicine mare's mane into her eyes. "I need shelter," she snapped.

Star kicked off in search of a less windy resting spot for the herd and the injured pegasus. The strange filly would need time to heal, if she survived at all. He saw a large rock in the distance, but it wasn't big enough to protect all the steeds from the wind. He returned to Sweetroot. "We'll have to shelter in the Trap."

Reluctantly, Sweetroot nodded. "Okay. Move her," she ordered. Two stallions each grabbed a wing and lifted the unconscious filly. Sweetroot trotted to the edge of the dark forest. The rest of River Herd followed.

The filly was laid out on her uninjured side. The helpers resumed the massaging and fanning. Sweetroot sent an apprentice to gather chickweed for the animal scratches, in case of infection.

Brackentail trotted forward for a closer look and gasped.

"What is it?" asked Thundersky.

"I know that filly," said Brackentail. "I can't believe she's here." His eyes were round with terror.

"Who is it?" asked Silverlake.

"It's Rockwing's daughter, Shadepebble."

"What? Are you sure?" asked Thundersky, grimacing.

Brackentail nodded. "I'm sure."

Panic blazed through River Herd. The steeds shuffled deeper into the Trap to hide themselves. "Can you wake her?" Dewberry asked Sweetroot.

"I'll try."

Star calmed the herd. "Listen," he neighed. "No over-stallion brings his yearling filly on a raid. I don't think Rockwing is here, and if he were, his army would have protected her from the animal that attacked her. This filly might belong to him, but I think she's alone."

"Maybe she's a refugee who's come to join us," suggested Morningleaf.

Brackentail shook his head, remembering his time with Mountain Herd after the canyon run. "No. She was happy. She wouldn't have left the Blue Mountains on her own."

"Then how do you think she got here?" asked Iceriver.

Brackentail looked perplexed. "I have no idea, but I agree with Star. Rockwing isn't with her. She was attacked, and she fell through the ice. These things would not have happened on Rockwing's watch." Brackentail took a deep breath. "But—"

"Go on," said Star.

"But that doesn't mean Rockwing isn't looking for her."

Dewberry nodded. "Of course he is. We can't keep her."

Morningleaf fluttered her feathers. "We can't abandon her either. She's hurt."

"Let's wait until she wakes up and then hear what she has to say," suggested Star.

"It's going to be a while," said Sweetroot. "She's out

cold, but I think she's going to live."

Thundersky tucked his crimson wings across his back. "We'll settle here for the night."

The River Herd steeds spent the rest of the day digging for lichen, grass, and roots. To Star's surprise, food was more plentiful in the Trap. The strange plants that had adapted to the dim light were protected from the heavy snow that covered the open tundra. It was warmer too, and the soil was not frozen. The thick ceiling of intertwined branches blocked in the heat of the creatures that lived there. Sweetroot left the injured filly's side to teach River Herd how to sample the foreign greenery for poisons before eating.

Star and his friends remained with Shadepebble. "This is Petalcloud's sister," whispered Morningleaf, examining the unconscious filly with intense interest. "She's just as pretty."

Star remembered hearing something about Shadepebble being born a dud, and a runt. He looked at the tiny, heavily spotted yearling lying on the forest floor, an almost exact replica of her silver sire except for her pink feathers. All that really mattered was that she was here, and her presence put River Herd in grave danger.

"I wonder if Shadepebble is as sour as Petalcloud?"

Dewberry asked, thinking aloud. "Look." She tugged on the filly. "One wing is shorter than the other. Maybe Rockwing banished her?"

Star looked closer at Shadepebble's wings and saw Dewberry was right. "We'll know soon enough," he said.

The days were still alarmingly short, and the sun had already passed the noon arc and was dropping toward the western horizon. While River Herd grazed on plants, Silverlake posted her sentries, and some of the yearlings went flying with Thundersky and Iceriver. Star stayed behind, wanting to heal the filly but knowing Sweetroot wouldn't want him to. Star and his friends surrounded Shadepebble to keep her warm.

Throughout the rest of the day, the filly had spurts of consciousness. She cried out with pain, and her legs scrambled as if she was running in her dreams.

"Maybe she was stolen from Mountain Herd," whispered Morningleaf, her eyes round with concern.

Star nodded. "Maybe." The day passed and half of the night. Star did not sleep, choosing to keep watch over the filly. She jerked and sometimes cried out. Every second she spent with River Herd put them in greater danger. If they were discovered with Shadepebble, it could be assumed that River Herd kidnapped her. And that would start a war.

Star glanced around and didn't see Sweetroot anywhere, so he decided to heal the filly. River Herd needed to know why she was in the north, and besides, her pain was intense. Star didn't think she'd be able to handle it when she woke. He would leave the scars on her body as proof that she'd been attacked by an animal and not by River Herd, in case she'd lost any of her memory and thought to accuse them.

Star shielded his head with his wings and called up his starfire, blowing it softly over Shadepebble like a warm breeze. Morningleaf woke, saw what he was doing, and encouraged him. "I was hoping you'd help her," she whispered.

After several minutes the filly opened her eyes. She was warm and perfect, except for the thick scars running down her flank. Star was pleased. Sweetroot had predicted the filly would live. He had just sped up the healing process.

Shadepebble startled when she became fully awake; her eyes were white rimmed and confused.

"You're safe," said Morningleaf, trying to calm her.

The spotted yearling fluttered her pink feathers. "When am I?"

"You mean 'where,' don't you?" said Dewberry.

Shadepebble struggled to her hooves, stared at her

healed scars, and blinked her eyes in disbelief. "No, I mean when. How long have I been asleep? When did you find me?"

"Earlier this same day," answered Morningleaf, baffled by the strange mare.

"But I'm healed," she exclaimed.

Morningleaf's eyes glowed. "Star did that."

"The black foal? Where is he?"

"He's right next to you," said Morningleaf.

Shadepebble swiveled her head and stared at Star, blinking as though she couldn't believe her eyes. "You healed me?"

Star nodded.

"Do you know who I am?"

"I do," said Star. "You're Rockwing's filly."

Her eyes bulged. "Yes. My father conquered your herd and tried to have you executed."

Star exhaled long and slow. "I know that, Shadepebble."

She gasped. "Of course—I'm sorry. . . . I just don't understand why you saved me. You could have let me drown and had revenge on my sire. I'm his last foal."

"Yes, I know that too."

The runt filly stared at him for a long time, but Star

saw her thoughts swimming rapidly through her eyes, schooling and scattering like fish. Finally she lowered her head and whispered, "My sire believes you'll claim Anok and destroy us. Is that true?"

Dewberry snorted. "He says that to scare you."

Star pawed the cold soil. "It's not true, Shadepebble, but you can believe what you want." He looked south, toward Mountain Herd's territory. "I've healed you; you're free to go."

She shook her head. "Can I stay, for a while." She glanced up at the leaves rustling in the wind. "I've been on an incredible journey since I was stolen from my herd. I've learned . . . well, I've learned that my sire has told me many lies. I'm not in a hurry to go home." She widened her dark eyes, and Star saw she was telling the truth, but he was also stunned that the daughter of an over-stallion like Rockwing wanted to stay with River Herd.

Morningleaf answered for him. "We have to speak to our council about that. Your sire will send an army for you. We don't want trouble."

Shadepebble nodded. "I understand."

"But how did you get here?" asked Morningleaf, changing the subject. "Who stole you?"

The yearling strained to stand. "I was kidnapped by Snow Herd raiders," she explained. "But after my sister recognized me, she banished the captain of the raid for making such a horrible mistake, and she sent me off with him. When my sire sends his warriors to get me back, Snow Herd will claim the captain acted on his own, as a stallion gone rogue." Her eyes brimmed with tears. "We've been wandering the north ever since."

"Where is this captain?" asked Star.

Shadepebble shivered. "I don't know. He saved me from an ice tiger that was chasing us. I kept running, and then I fell through the ice."

Morningleaf stroked Shadepebble's back. "You're safe now."

Shadepebble looked at Star. "I can still feel your power working inside me, keeping me warm." Shadepebble lowered her head, her eyes heavy with sleep.

"You're exhausted," commented Morningleaf. "You should rest."

"Thank you," Shadepebble nickered, soon falling asleep.

Star stood watch over Shadepebble, his thoughts in a jumble. The daughter of his worst enemy now trusted him because he'd been gentle with her and healed her. It was similar to how he'd gained the trust of the bird Crabwing. He'd fed the gull and treated him gently. If only the pegasi of Anok allowed him to help them, they would surrender their fears and unite. He was sure of it.

19

UPSIDE DOWN

AFTER ARRIVING AT THE SOUTHERNMOST EDGE of the Trap, Frostfire's team had to shelter for three days while a terrible blizzard passed through. Frostfire was still upset they had not found Shadepebble with Snow Herd. He wondered how Rockwing would react when he failed to return the overstallion's last surviving filly. It made the mission of capturing Morningleaf that much more important. He could fail once—maybe—but he could not fail twice. Rockwing would banish him, or worse. Frostfire sighed, feeling overwhelmed.

"Frostfire, come see this!" cried Larksong.

His blood raced at the alarming tone of her voice, and he flew toward her. She stood on a patch of melted snow near the edge of the Trap. Sprawled at her hooves was one of his stallions.

Frostfire landed. "What is it?"

Larksong backed away, her eyes round. "His tongue! Look at his tongue. It's blue."

Frostfire's small team panicked at the sight of the blue roan warrior lying on his side, coughing. Sweat beaded and rolled down his hide. "I'm fine," he rasped.

Frostfire flew up and hovered over him. "Get back!" he whinnied to his team. "You too," he neighed at Larksong. Frostfire's thoughts tumbled. His mission was swirling out of reach. They were probably all infected.

He glanced at Larksong. Her black eyes were desperate. "What do we do?" she cried.

"Just get away from him," he said. "All of you." His team flew toward the lake about a mile away. Frostfire gazed at the wheezing stallion. "How long have you been sick?" he asked.

"My throat's hurt since we spied on Snow Herd. I didn't . . . I had no idea it was the plague. I thought it was the cold weather."

The stallion's mouth hung open, and his tongue lolled out, swollen and blue. His eyes were fever bright. Frostfire knew that if the plague didn't kill him, the sweating would. The stallion's coat was wet, and the cold air would soon freeze him to death. Spastic shivers ran through the warrior's body at intervals. He thrashed, but he did not have the energy to rise. "Don't leave me here. Please."

Frostfire's throat tightened. This was his warrior, and he did not want to leave him to die alone in the snow, but his team could not risk staying near him, nor spend weeks trying to heal him. "Don't plead with me," he said to the roan. "I can't save you. I want to, but I can't. I can't even stay near you."

The stallion closed his mouth, understanding.

"I can speed your journey to the golden meadow," Frostfire offered, coiling back his sharpened hoof.

The stallion rolled his eyes toward Frostfire. "No. Once I rest, I'll be able to get up. I'll make it home on my own."

Frostfire nodded, feeling proud of the stallion's determination, even though they both knew he would not make it home. "I'm sorry," Frostfire said, and meant it. He hated to lose a warrior.

Frostfire flew away and joined his team. "It's the Blue Tongue plague," he said to them.

Larksong snapped her jaws shut. "I'm not going to die in this miserable place," she said. "Not from some dumb plague, and not before we steal that filly from Star." She twisted her head to look at Frostfire. "The storm is over. What's the plan? How are we going to get her? The black foal keeps her close."

Frostfire grimaced. Again he was taken aback by the boldness of her questions. As a captain, he wasn't used to them. He had to remind himself she was a sky herder, not a warrior, and she didn't know any better. "When it's time, I'll give you your orders," he said.

Larksong leaned in close to him, staring into his eyes. Her wing brushed his. "You don't *have* a plan, do you?"

Her touch startled him and rendered him speechless. He felt trapped by her intense gaze and the heady scent of her long mane. He said nothing, his mind spinning.

Larksong huffed and broke eye contact.

Frostfire trotted away from her to collect himself. She was utterly fearless of him—unlike the rest of his team. He could kill her for talking back to her captain during a mission; surely she knew that even though she was a sky herder. Frostfire tossed his mane, baffled by her and her words because, as usual, she was right. He didn't have a plan. He was hoping one would present itself once he found the River Herd steeds. The best idea he'd come up with so far was to create a distraction and then whisk

Morningleaf away. But he had no idea how he would accomplish that. Not yet.

He glanced at the sky, which was pale blue and full of puffy white clouds; it wasn't going to snow today. With or without a plan, it was time to get moving. "We'll travel along the edge of the Trap, heading north, until we reach the Hoofbeat Mountains."

His team flexed their wings for flight.

"It will take us several days to reach the end of the woods," he explained. "Then we'll be in the Ice Lands, and we'll only fly at night. River Herd could be anywhere."

"Or they could be right in front of us," said Larksong, looking smug.

"What?" Frostfire whipped around to find Star, Thundersky, and the rest of River Herd staring at him from a mile away. Standing next to the black foal was the target of his mission: Morningleaf. And if all this wasn't shocking enough, next to her was Brackentail, the yearling colt he'd left for dead. Behind him was Frostfire's sire, Iceriver.

Frostfire gulped, driving air into his tight lungs, and dropped his wings in defeat. His head swam with questions. River Herd was supposed to be in the Ice Lands; what were they doing heading south? And why were there so few of them? Maybe they too had succumbed to the plague.

There was nothing to do now but confront them. He reminded himself that he had an excuse to be here: he was searching for Shadepebble. Frostfire led his team across the snow, and they halted a short distance from River Herd. Iceriver neighed a short, joyful greeting. Frostfire hadn't seen his sire since the day of his weaning, but he did not return the greeting. Anger sizzled through his veins at the sight of Iceriver. His sire had not stopped Petalcloud from trading him, and that fact would always be a thorn between them.

Brackentail pinned his ears, and Frostfire swept his eyes over the brown yearling. The injuries he'd given Brackentail before banishing him were healed. The black foal must have used his powers on him, because Frostfire remembered breaking one of those orange wings permanently.

Frostfire's gaze landed on Star. He'd grown taller since his birthday. It seemed ages ago that Frostfire had snatched the dud colt by his useless wings and carried him off to meet Rockwing for the first time. Now the dud could fly, and he could easily kill Frostfire with a huff of his breath.

Star broke the silence. "I assume you've come for Shadepebble."

Frostfire's limp wings flared at the mention of his aunt's name. *Was Shadepebble with River Herd?* Stunned, but not wanting to appear ignorant, he just nodded.

Star whistled, and Frostfire watched Shadepebble trot through a group of pegasi and stand next to the black foal, so close to him that their shoulders touched. She was clearly *not* his captive.

Frostfire's thoughts spun, unraveling and re-forming as he adjusted to the sight of his aunt. Shadepebble was the last pegasus he'd expected to see here. And she was alive! Frostfire hadn't failed either mission, not yet. He'd found both fillies, and River Herd could not be suspicious of him. They had his aunt—they were the ones who looked suspicious.

Frostfire spoke, knowing his team would follow his lead. "Yes, we're a rescue party." He willed his eyes not to look at Morningleaf, not to give away his true intentions. "Shadepebble was taken from us by Snow Herd. We've been searching Anok for her. How is it you have her?" Frostfire rattled his feathers.

"We found her," said Thundersky, also rattling his feathers. "She was drowning, and Star saved her."

Frostfire blinked, confused. Star saved an enemy steed? He took a deep breath and looked at Shadepebble. "Is this true?"

The undersize filly nodded. "Yes. And I'd like to stay with them. With River Herd."

"What?" Frostfire's fragile sense of order collapsed. *His aunt didn't want to come home?* His eyes scanned River Herd—from Iceriver and Thundersky, who'd given up being over-stallions to follow Star; to Brackentail, who'd been accepted back into the herd he had once betrayed; to Star, who had the power to rule Anok but who lived like a nomadic land horse; and then to his own deformed aunt, who was ready to abandon her herd. When had the world turned upside down?

"Excuse us," said Frostfire. He snatched Shadepebble's wing in his jaws and dragged her aside. "You are an embarrassment to your sire," he hissed, staring into her determined eyes. "You will come home now."

"You're hurting me," she said, her eyes wide.

Frostfire groaned. "I'm confused. Did you run away, or were you kidnapped? Hedgewind told me you flew for your life."

"I was taken," stammered Shadepebble. "But when Snow Herd found out who I was, they banished me and the captain—Clawfire—who took me. He and I became friends. We set out to look for Star. I'm here by choice."

"Where is this captain?" rasped Frostfire.

"I don't know. We were attacked by an ice tiger, and then I ran and broke through a frozen pond. Star saved me."

Frostfire threw up his wings. "They're all manipulating you, Shadepebble. You're the filly of an over-stallion; you're a hostage."

Shadepebble stamped her hoof into the crisp snow. "No! They said I could leave if I wanted. All my life I've been told that foreign steeds are evil, but they aren't. Rockwing lied. He lied to the whole herd!"

Frostfire collected his thoughts. Shadepebble felt indebted to Star—it was a powerful obligation for a pegasus, one he wouldn't be able to argue her out of, but he tried anyway. "Do you realize, Shadepebble, that you wouldn't have been attacked by an ice tiger if you hadn't been kidnapped in the first place? You don't owe anyone for saving you from an attack that should never have happened."

Shadepebble clenched her jaws and pinned her ears, but said nothing.

Frostfire closed his eyes. Rockwing didn't argue with irrational steeds, and neither would he. "I'm taking you home." He nodded to his team, and they seized her, ready to take her by force.

Star and Thundersky reared, galloping closer, ready to fight, and Shadepebble whinnied, throwing open her small wings to stop the altercation. "Okay, okay! Please don't fight!" Shadepebble staggered sideways, almost falling over.

"What's wrong with you?" snapped Frostfire.

"I'm just very tired and hungry," she replied. "Please let me rest, and think, and then I'll come with you on my own."

Frostfire thought about it. Staying to let Shadepebble rest would give him more time to plan the kidnapping of Morningleaf. He folded his wings and said, "I will give you one day and one night to rest. After that we go home."

Shadepebble let out her breath. "That's all I need."

Frostfire turned to Star. "My team will camp there," he said, pointing toward a clump of fir trees. "Will you accept a truce with us while we wait for Shadepebble to recover?"

Star glanced at Thundersky and Silverlake, who nodded.

"You may stay," Star said, and then he caught Thundersky's attention. "I'm going to patrol the area, to make sure the ice tiger isn't still lurking near. Will you keep the herd close together until I know that it's moved on and that we're safe?"

Thundersky nodded, and the black foal turned and galloped into the sky, followed by Morningleaf, Silverlake, and twelve others. Frostfire watched his aqua-feathered prize pierce a cloud and disappear. But soon Morningleaf would return, and he would be waiting.

20

THE TRUTH

STAR DIVIDED HIS STEEDS INTO TWO GROUPS. ONE would soar over the woods and one over the tundra. If the ice tiger were still around, they could probably scare it off. Most cats were skittish when confronted, and he hoped the same was true for the large, long-fanged tigers of the north. Morningleaf followed Dewberry's group, and Silverlake stayed with Star. They dropped from the sky often to inspect the snow for tiger prints, but found no sign of the beast. They'd all just returned to River Herd when a spasm of pain shot through Star's mind.

"Ack!" His wings tensed and his feathers curled, causing Star to crash into the snow.

Silverlake and her sentries landed next to him, and

the River Herd steeds galloped closer. Silverlake's ears swiveled, listening for danger, and her breath came faster. "What is it?" She glanced west, searching the sky. Ever since he'd told her about Nightwing, she'd been on edge.

Star grabbed his head in his wings. His eyes rolled back, and his body twitched. One half of his mind was conscious enough to be embarrassed that he was rolling in the snow, grunting and thrashing. The other half was far away, cruising fast and low over the ocean, heading west. He was caught in the grip of another vision, but this time he was awake!

His starfire gurgled to life in response to the pain in his head. Star smelled salt. His spirit body glided over the sea, and his hooves dipped into the water, making a long, gentle ripple.

His spirit was off to visit Nightwing again. But why? Had the dark stallion called him, or was Star at the mercy of his starfire, a power he still didn't understand?

Ahead was Nightwing, flying toward him, his hooves also skimming the sea—and it was like Star was watching himself. But this black pegasus had no white star, and he was bone thin and dull coated. Nightwing glided effortlessly, carried by the wind currents, and he approached Star with his teeth bared. Star trumpeted in alarm, and then the stallion passed through his spirit body—toward Anok—leaving Star colder than the snow.

Star heard Silverlake's nervous whinny through his dream. "Get back!" she warned the watching steeds, sensing the tension building in Star.

Star kicked wildly and then rolled onto his hooves, pawing at the ice with hot steam pouring from his nose, and his hooves glowing gold. Silverlake and the others were blurry shapes standing around him. He struggled to focus his eyes, and his body tensed with the need to fight, or run. He spun in a circle, looking for the haggard stallion with the silver eyes, but Nightwing was nowhere. Star opened his mouth and blasted the snow around him with golden fire. It melted, revealing fresh green lichen and gray rocks.

Then the world suddenly snapped into focus and Star groaned, reeling sideways.

"Star! What happened?" asked Silverlake, creeping toward him, her ears flat and wary. "What did you see?"

Star shivered. He was positive his vision had shown him the actions of Nightwing in real time. The four-hundred-year-old stallion was traveling fast, heading toward Anok. "He's on his way here," gasped Star.

"No!" she whinnied, twirling around. The River Herd

steeds stared at them, baffled. "It's time you told them," said Silverlake.

Star nodded and raised his voice to address all the pegasi. "Since I received my starfire, I've been sensing Nightwing's presence. He's alive. I believe he's been hibernating across the sea." Star took a deep breath and continued. "But he's awake now, and he's returning to Anok. I've waited to say something, hoping I was wrong, hoping it was just my new powers that I was getting used to. But Nightwing is heading toward us as we speak."

The fierce bravado of the pegasi melted like spring snowflakes, and many voices cried out at once:

"The destroyer?"

"No."

"What will we do?"

Thundersky threw back his head and trumpeted the alarm of an over-stallion.

From the clump of trees, Frostfire heard the commotion and led his team toward them. "What's happening?" he asked. His warriors pawed the snow, their muscles trembling for battle.

Star reared and slammed down his hooves—drawing everyone's attention. "It's true," he said, sweeping his eyes over the panicking pegasi. "Nightwing is awake."

Frostfire's jaw dropped.

"But we have time to prepare," said Star, trying to calm them. "He's across the Great Sea, but he's flying this way."

"What does he want?" asked Frostfire.

Star lowered his head, feeling miserable to upset his herd. "Probably me."

Dewberry snorted. "Or to finish what he started four hundred years ago."

Star shot her a sharp glance.

"I'm just saying what we're all thinking," she whinnied.

Four hundred years ago Nightwing set out to destroy the pegasi of Anok. Only because of the ancient stallion Spiderwing had any steeds survived.

"She's right, I think," said Iceriver. "It makes sense. A new black foal is a threat to the old one."

Thundersky nodded, and Star sighed. Of course the two past over-stallions understood rivalry better than most steeds.

"Nightwing can't cross the ocean in a day," said Star. "And he's weak, probably from sleeping for so long. We have time to think, to plan."

The pegasi grumbled and shed feathers onto the snow.

"Listen to Star," said Thundersky.

Star was grateful for Thundersky's support. "First, we must warn the other herds," he said.

This caused more heated murmuring in River Herd.

"But how will we fight him?" asked Frostfire, lashing his tail.

"*We* won't," said Star. "*I* will."

Frostfire eyed him doubtfully. "You don't have an army. You'll need one if you hope to defeat him."

"An army will slow me down."

Frostfire lifted his head. "You're arrogant, black foal. How could you fight a powerful pegasus like Nightwing on your own? You'll get yourself killed—you'll get us all killed. You'll destroy Anok!"

Star sighed and dropped the argument. It was true; Nightwing had destroyed an army of tens of thousands with ease, but Star had no intentions of letting that happen again. He had the silver fire, just like Nightwing. He'd killed the bear with it. He could fight the Destroyer.

"Stop arguing," said Sweetroot, stepping forward. "Don't you see this could be the end of us?"

Silverlake gasped. "Don't say that."

Sweetroot unfolded and refolded her wings. "Slathering the truth with honey won't change it," she said. "Nightwing is coming to destroy us all. For once in our blasted lives, the herds of Anok need to stop fighting one another and unite."

Loud muttering erupted among the gathered steeds.

"The council of River Herd will meet to discuss this," said Thundersky.

The herd disbanded, breaking off in small groups, their eyes trained on the sky. Nothing ferocious had ever come at them from above. The sky was their domain, but not any longer.

Star trotted to the pond to drink and think. With Nightwing on his way, Star worried about Morning-leaf. The Destroyer had seen her face, and had killed her in Star's dream. But besides her safety, Star had a secret from Morningleaf—one he'd only shared with Silverlake—that he was *also* a destroyer. Morningleaf had seen a glimpse of it when he'd healed Brackentail's wing, but they hadn't spoken of it since.

Now Star was counting on that ugly power to fight Nightwing, and he would have to tap into his darkest feelings, his anger and bitterness. Star took a deep breath. He didn't want Morningleaf to see him that way.

Like a spirit, Morningleaf materialized beside him, jolting Star from his thoughts. "Are you afraid?" she asked.

He looked at her dainty chestnut face, wide blaze, and

flaxen forelock. Her amber eyes were soft tonight, her aqua wings relaxed.

"I am," he said.

She nickered, and the gentle sound soothed him. "So am I, but it's going to be okay."

Star inhaled, taking his first deep breath since the vision overtook his mind. "You don't know that."

"I do."

"But how? You can't."

She tucked her muzzle against his chest. "I have visions too."

Star gaped at her. "You do? What have you seen?"

She lifted her head and smoothed his ruffled feathers. "The future," she said. "All the herds living together in a valley of long grass. United."

Star gasped. "That's the golden meadow, Morningleaf. You've seen the end, not the future."

"I don't think so," she said.

Star hadn't meant to challenge her. "Was I there?"

Morningleaf closed her eyes. "No, but I probably just didn't see you."

Star tugged her mane gently. "Is this you trying to make me feel better?"

She nickered. "Sorry."

"Don't be. I have the starfire. Nightwing can't take over like he did last time. I can fight him, and I will win."

Morningleaf snuggled closer to him, and they each closed their eyes as night fell in the north.

21

ESCORT

THE NEXT DAY THE RIVER HERD COUNCIL MET. Since Nightwing was a problem that belonged to all of Anok, Frostfire, Shadepebble, and every River Herd steed was invited to attend the meeting. The members stood in a circle and discussed their options regarding Nightwing's return, their breaths coming out as puffs of steam against the hazy glow of the sun.

Frostfire wanted to speak to his sire, Iceriver, but hadn't had the opportunity. Now here they were, facing each other, still not free to speak. His memories of his sire were few. Iceriver had avoided Frostfire when he was a foal. Perhaps because he knew he couldn't keep his colt. Years later, after Petalcloud had traded him to Rockwing,

Frostfire heard that Iceriver had sired a filly named Lightfeather with another mare. Petalcloud had driven that foal from Snow Herd too, and Frostfire didn't know what had happened to Lightfeather after that.

Frostfire caught his sire's eye across the circle. Iceriver seemed to want to speak to him too, but then he looked away. Frostfire chewed his lip. They were from enemy herds—and that complicated things.

Bumblewind interrupted the discussion. "Why don't we gather an army to fight Nightwing?"

"Because *I* will fight Nightwing," Star reminded him.

Frostfire studied the young black stallion, remembering when Star was a foal and Frostfire had snatched him from Feather Lake. Star had just been beaten up and almost drowned by two colts. He wasn't much of a fighter then.

Looking at him now, Frostfire saw Star was thoughtful, and in close quarters he was also intimidating. He was built like a warrior, but controlled his temper. His voice was quiet and deep, but rumbled like thunder. His eyes were large and soft, but deep inside they flickered, like he was about to catch fire. A steady hum of starfire crackled inside his body, and Frostfire had no doubt Star could execute all of Mountain Herd as easily as he breathed. Perhaps he really could fight the Destroyer on his own.

Frostfire wondered if it was wise of Rockwing to provoke Star by kidnapping Morningleaf. He didn't think so, but he understood that Rockwing wouldn't claim Sun Herd's territory any other way. Everything had changed now that Star had his power, and the Sun Herd territory was Star's birthland, the home of his mother's grave, and Star was no longer a powerless colt. But Star's fierce attachment to Morningleaf had been made clear to all on his birthday, and she was his only known weakness. Frostfire glanced at the little chestnut filly. He needed to get her and Shadepebble, and get out. Fast.

Star continued speaking, his words breaking into Frostfire's thoughts. "I think the herds should hide from Nightwing in the Trap." Star shifted from hoof to hoof, and Frostfire glimpsed his uncertainty. "I almost ran away there once, when I was a weanling. It's perfect."

"The Trap?" Silverlake whinnied. "Nightwing could set it on fire."

"True," said Star, "but he won't know pegasi are hiding there. You won't be visible from the sky or from the ground. The forest ceiling is too thick with branches, and the trees are so close together that visibility disappears after several winglengths. The Trap is large enough to hide every steed in Anok. And if he sets it on fire, you aren't stuck in it like you would be in a cave or canyon. You can run out any side of it."

"It's not a bad idea," nickered Sweetroot.

"We can suggest it to the other herds when we warn them about Nightwing," said Silverlake. "We should send messengers today."

"What if the other herds don't want to hide?" asked Bumblewind.

Star shrugged his wings. "Then at least we tried to help them."

Frostfire listened to the exchanges between the council. Discussing plans was no way to lead a herd, especially a frightened one. But he agreed with Star: hiding in the Trap was a good idea.

Silverlake spoke. "I'll prepare the messengers. The rest of us can wait here, at the edge of the Trap. We'll greet and settle the herds when they arrive, and organize them into camps to prevent fighting."

"But what about Snow Herd?" asked Bumblewind. "They're still affected by the plague."

Heavy silence fell on the council. "He's right," said Thundersky. "Inviting Snow Herd would lead to mass infection, especially with all of us living so close together."

Frostfire cringed, wondering if his team was carrying

and spreading the plague. Then he looked at Star. Could the black foal heal plagues? He probably could; he'd healed Brackentail's ruined wing. Frostfire's thoughts drifted to his sick warrior. What if Star could heal him? Frostfire chewed his lip. No. He would never ask Star for help, and by now his stallion had to be dead, killed by the ice tiger or some other predator, or frozen to death. Frostfire returned his attention to the council meeting.

"Are you suggesting we don't warn them?" Silverlake asked, wrapping her wings tightly around her chest.

Sweetroot slumped. "We can't leave them to fend for themselves."

"It's their own doing," Dewberry reminded everyone. "I was there. They could have let Star heal them."

Frostfire pricked his ears. Star had tried to heal Snow Herd? Was the black foal looking to make a pact, to save Snow Herd so they'd volunteer their own enslavement to him? Frostfire's heart tripped forward, skipping beats. Star was more dangerous than anyone suspected, perhaps even more cunning than Nightwing. He eyed the young black stallion warily.

Star flung his heavy mane to the other side of his neck. "Snow Herd refused my help out of fear of me, Thundersky; please don't punish them for that. The Trap is big enough for us to spread out. They can take the southwestern corner and quarantine themselves there. Will that keep us safe, Sweetroot?"

"I think so," she said, her eyes softening.

Frostfire wanted to bray at them all. *Didn't they see how Star had poisoned their minds?* The black foal had them all convinced he was good, but Frostfire saw how they lived—homeless, leaderless, half-starved, and vulnerable to predators—and Star's herd accepted these miserable conditions. They were delusional—living under Star's control—and even Shadepebble had succumbed to it. Frostfire was anxious to leave, to get his team away from the black foal before his evil influence turned them all into slaves.

The council nodded to one another, and Star called the vote. The decision to hide in the Trap and send messengers to all the herds was unanimous.

"There is one more matter to consider," said Star, taking a breath so deep his ribs rattled. He looked at the blue-winged filly and winced as he spoke. "You're not safe. I need a volunteer to hide you from me."

Morningleaf threw her head up. "What? Why?"

"I believe Nightwing will use you against me," said Star.

Frostfire exhaled slowly, hiding his excitement. This was his opportunity! If they separated Morningleaf from Star, he could snatch her.

"No," said Morningleaf, flaring her wings. "I won't go."

"For once I think we're safer apart," said Star.

Morningleaf narrowed her eyes and lashed her tail. Frostfire watched her, noticing that the black foal had upset her.

"Nightwing saw your face in one of Star's visions," Silverlake explained to her filly, trying to calm her. "Star and I are worried about you."

"Then I'll hide in the Trap with everyone else."

Star interrupted. "No. I can't know where you are. Not as long as Nightwing and I are connected. He'll find you through me."

"I'll hide her," said Thundersky.

Morningleaf stomped the snow. "No. If you want me to leave, I'll hide myself." She glared at Star. "But I don't agree with it."

"You can't travel alone," said Star.

"I'll go with her," said Frostfire, trying not to appear eager.

Every steed stared at him as though they'd forgotten he was standing there, but they listened, their ears swiveling nervously.

Frostfire explained. "You saved Shadepebble's life, and Rockwing ordered me not to return without his filly. If Star hadn't saved her and healed her, I would be banished for life. I will escort your filly in exchange for that." Frostfire dared not look at his team, who stood nearby and knew he was lying. "Besides, I know the perfect place where she can hide. It's not big enough for all the herds, but it will work for her, and I can promise you that Nightwing won't find her there."

The council considered his offer. "It's in Frostfire's best interest to help us," said Sweetroot. "And we can't risk Nightwing getting hold of Morningleaf. We all know how Star feels about her. If Frostfire can take her to this secret place, she'll be safe from whatever comes next."

Frostfire watched Star react to that. He appeared surprised and embarrassed at the medicine mare's words, but he didn't deny them, and that was good.

"Who's in favor?" asked Silverlake.

Morningleaf raised her wing. "Please, Mama, don't vote about this," she said. "If I stay or go, it's my decision, not yours." She turned to Frostfire, glaring at him as if she had her own starfire and would blast him with it. "You can show me this hiding place, but I want my own team."

Thundersky turned to his filly. "I'll help you choose the

best warriors." He threw a menacing glance at Frostfire.

She nodded, and Frostfire was amazed this herd functioned at all. Where was the leadership? Rockwing would never allow a yearling to make decisions.

It was agreed that Frostfire's and Morningleaf's teams would leave that very afternoon.

22

GOOD-BYE

SILVERLAKE CHOSE FOUR STEEDS TO WARN DES-
ert Herd, Jungle Herd, Snow Herd, and Mountain Herd
about Nightwing's eminent return. She also selected a
messenger to find Hazelwind and his followers. They left
immediately.

Star folded his wings and watched Frostfire gather his
team, joined by Morningleaf. She and Thundersky had
selected Iceriver and three River Herd stallions to accom-
pany her to the hiding place. The afternoon was crisp and
calm, the bright sun reflected off the melting ice, and the
heavily trampled snow around them had turned to slush.
Morningleaf preened her feathers, taking delicate care
with the ends, and Star caught her gaze across the backs

of a dozen steeds. She pricked her ears. To him, she'd never looked so small, or so brave.

Star closed his eyes, remembering the day her sire broke her neck by mistake. Star had cringed as he saw Morningleaf's body topple off the plateau. She'd landed in a crumpled heap on the grass, her head facing the wrong way. The memories caused his heart to pound, and his feelings threatened to choke him.

No pegasus in Anok meant more to him than Morningleaf, and her devotion to him was absolute, like Lightfeather's had been. He searched his heart for the reason, comparing her to every pegasus he knew, and he quickly found his answer: Morningleaf *believed* he was the healer; the rest of them just *hoped* he was. The difference meant everything to Star, and he thrived off her unwavering faith in him. Besides that, he believed in her too. Morningleaf was free of doubt or fear. She cared about the steeds of Anok, every single one, down to their last feather. He couldn't say the same about anyone else, not even himself.

Star heard the echo of Grasswing's voice in his mind. *We have nothing to lose for gaining you, Star*, he'd said. Misery and grief squeezed his heart at the memory. Star had looked up to Grasswing like a sire. He missed his presence, his wise words that were always comforting. Star had not forgiven Rockwing for killing the old palomino stallion, and the bitterness of it was powerful. Star knew he should turn from his anger; but anger made his starfire destructive, and anger was what he needed to defeat Nightwing.

Star opened his eyes. Morningleaf had flown across the snow and was standing right in front of him, studying his face. "Soaking up the sun?" she asked, her eyes warm and twinkling.

"Sure," he said.

She knocked him in the shoulder with her wing. "We both know you were worrying."

"No, I—" *Could she read his thoughts?*

"Thanks a lot for shuffling me off with that toad," she said, pointing her wing at Frostfire.

"You agreed to go," he reminded her.

She huffed. "Not really. I would rather stay with you."

"You understand why that's not a good idea, right?"

She smirked. "Let me guess; you don't want a repeat of last time—when I had to save your life."

"I think I saved *your* life," Star teased back.

"I saved yours first."

"We're even then."

"Nope," she nickered. "I want the last life saving."

He bumped her hip with his. "You're so competitive."

She gazed at him, her eyes blazing. "No one here understands you like I do. You're going to be all alone."

"I know." He dropped his muzzle to hers. They both knew it was the same for Morningleaf. No one understood her like he did. She would be alone too, even surrounded by her team.

Silverlake and Thundersky interrupted them. "It's time to go," Silverlake said to her filly.

The joy on Morningleaf's face evaporated.

Thundersky wrapped his bloodred wings around her, and the sight gave Star a chill. "Stay close to Iceriver," he said. "I don't trust Frostfire."

Morningleaf scowled. "You shouldn't!"

Silverlake tried to placate her filly and her mate. "Iceriver will protect you, and Frostfire owes Star for saving Shadepebble's life. He won't harm you."

Morningleaf nodded. "I know. I'm not afraid of him."

Star watched his best friend prepare to leave, and a fresh feeling of doom descended on him like the crushing blow of a hoof. "Maybe we should reconsider," he said, trying to squash his sudden panic.

"We're out of time, Star," nickered Silverlake. "They

need to go. She'll be safe with Iceriver and the three stallions I chose." Iceriver was the most experienced warrior in Anok, and still mightily powerful.

But the terrible feeling still clutched at Star's heart, not letting go. Star vibrated his wings and was shocked when black feathers dropped from them and stuck in the snow. He'd never shed feathers before! But with Nightwing getting closer to Anok each day and Morningleaf leaving him, his flesh tingled like it was crawling with sand bugs. He had a crazy idea. "We should send one more steed with her," he said. "Brackentail."

"Brackentail?" whinnied Morningleaf, her eyes widening. "Why?"

Star flipped his long forelock out of his eyes, knowing his request didn't make sense. He tried to explain. "Of all the steeds in Anok, none will keep a closer eye on you than Brackentail." Star looked around as the truth of his words settled on Morningleaf's parents.

"He's right," said Thundersky to his filly. "Every stupid thing that colt has done has been for you."

Star closed his eyes, remembering how true that was. When Brackentail tried to kill him in the canyon run, he'd said he was doing it for Morningleaf. Star hadn't understood at the time, but Brackentail had been trying to protect her. He'd been protecting her since they were foals. Star opened his eyes and glanced at Morningleaf, understanding that Brackentail's devotion to her matched his own.

Morningleaf fluttered her wings, looking upset for the first time. "Star?" she said, questioning him, her amber eyes confused. "Do you really want me traveling with Brackentail?" Her question was loaded with unspoken feelings and memories.

Yes and no, thought Star, conflicted. What he wanted was for Morningleaf and him to stay together, but since that wasn't possible, he wanted a steed with her who loved Morningleaf as much as he did. He wished it could be himself, but it would have to be Brackentail. "Brackentail will do anything for you . . . like I would," Star answered. "Please take him with you."

Morningleaf trotted to Star and buried her nose in his mane. "If you want me to, I will," she whispered.

And Star was glad she trusted him. He curled his neck around hers. "When all this is over, meet me where the birds don't fly." It was their secret code for the little beach at Crabwing's Bay.

Morningleaf nodded. "I will," she said, her voice wavering as tears dampened her cheeks. She didn't ask what he meant by *over*, and Star was glad, because he didn't know.

Morningleaf said her final good-byes, and they all tried not to cry, even Dewberry. Morningleaf gathered her team and they left. Star held his breath as he watched his best friend lift into the sky, flapping her perfectly formed wings. Her chestnut body gleamed bright, reflecting the sun, and her flaxen tail streamed behind her like golden stems of wheat. Iceriver, Brackentail, her three guardian stallions, and Frostfire's team joined her, forming a large V, flying south. Morningleaf didn't look back.

Star noticed that Frostfire did not look pleased at the reinforcements, especially the addition of his sire, Iceriver. But Star felt suddenly relieved, his terrible dread soothed. He let out his breath. Morningleaf would survive whatever happened next.

But Star felt empty.

Thundersky faced him, looking equally heartbroken. "How will you prepare for Nightwing?" he asked Star.

"I'm going to fly to the Hoofbeat Mountains and practice using my starfire. I won't be able to hurt anyone up on the peaks, by myself."

"I'll stay with you," said Thundersky. "I'm not afraid."

Star appraised the bay stallion who'd once been Star's worst enemy. There was no trace of the old days in

Thundersky now. "No offense, but you can't help me."

Thundersky was silent for a long time. Star grew uneasy; worried he'd offended him. Finally the stallion spoke. His voice was rough, his eyes full of pain. "I'm sorry . . . for everything," he said.

Star's head flew up so fast he felt dizzy. In the history of Anok, he doubted any over-stallion had ever apologized for anything. Star didn't know what to say.

Thundersky took a deep breath and let it out slowly, then he trotted away to join Silverlake and the others who were staking out a home in the Trap. After a few steps he turned and bowed his head to Star, ever so slightly, then he kicked off, coasting over the icy snow, his crimson feathers swirling behind him like petals off an old rose.

Star's mind and heart raced while his hooves stood rooted in the snow. This day was the strangest in many moons. He gazed at his loyal friends. They had left the security of their herds to follow him, and protect him, but now their lives were in his wings alone. The weight of it both anchored and uplifted him at the same time. He watched their earnest faces and saw them each as weanlings—fragile, innocent, vulnerable. Star would do whatever he could to keep them safe.

With the world padded in snow and the wind calm,

Star swiveled his ears. The silence was absolute—no bugs, no swishing of grass, no birds, no breathing but his own. *Was he so small, or was Anok so large?*

Star galloped as fast as he could, expelling his stress, racing like he was a foal again. His legs blurred and his neck rocked to the rhythm of his hoofbeats, and then he pushed off and lifted into the blue heights. His gut trilled as he rose higher and higher, until the horizon bowed and he was far above the clouds. In the distance he could see the flying bodies of Frostfire and Morningleaf as they departed the Ice Lands.

Star landed on the highest peak and faced west. The fierce and chilly wind battered him, and the air here was thin and dry. In the distance, black smoke drifted across the ocean. Somewhere on the Great Sea, maybe on an island, a fire raged. Star pricked his ears forward. The dark force of Nightwing yanked at his thoughts, growing stronger. Star turned toward a large boulder on his left and let his anger loose, and formed a silver fireball. He hurled it at the rock, exploding it to ash. Satisfied, he curled into a pocket of snow to sleep. He would practice with the destructive fire, and when Nightwing arrived, he would be ready.

23

FRIENDS

MORNINGLEAF GLIDED ON A FAST WAKE, DODGING moist clouds as she trailed Frostfire. Her team flew beside her and they were all traveling south, but she had no idea where. Star believed he was protecting her by asking her to hide, but she disagreed. They were stronger and safer together, and leaving Star had cored out a hollow pit in the center of her heart. She'd only gone along with this plan because it was clear her presence distracted *him*. It was for *his* safety, not hers that she left. She flew in silence, trying not to think about it.

The arctic sun warmed Morningleaf's feathers, and she noticed birds singing in the trees. Ground squirrels poked out of their holes, sniffing the air and venturing hesitantly onto the snow. The delicious scent of sprouting plants reached her in the sky. There was a feeling of peacefulness in the north that soothed Morningleaf, a sort of gratitude for each day that lingered between the hard-won hours. Perhaps it was because the climate was so brutally unforgiving, or perhaps the gratitude sprang from Morningleaf herself, from her quiet joy that Star had made it to his first birthday and was still alive.

But in spite of her gratitude, Morningleaf watched Frostfire and his team warily. She didn't trust the powerful stallion who'd beaten up Brackentail, an inexperienced yearling, and broken his wing. It was the type of nastiness she expected from a Mountain Herd steed, and so she was thankful Iceriver and the three River Herd stallions were along to protect her. She was not so appreciative of Brackentail himself. She often caught him staring at her feathers, and it made her uncomfortable; but Star had accepted him, and Brackentail seemed truly sorry for the things he'd done when they were weanlings.

Next to Frostfire flew his father, Iceriver. Morningleaf noticed the two steeds had matching ringlets in their tails. The two stallions talked quietly, and their words drifted with the wind so Morningleaf couldn't hear what they were saying.

Then Frostfire raised his voice and spoke over his shoulder. "We'll stop at Mountain Herd's northern border. One of my stallions will escort Shadepebble the rest of the way home."

The little dappled filly, Shadepebble, broke the V formation and sidled next to Morningleaf. "Want some company?"

Morningleaf brightened. "Sure." She glanced at Shadepebble's little wing, which had to flap so much faster than her longer one. "Do you want to draft off me?" Morningleaf asked.

Shadepebble gasped, looking offended, but quickly shook it off. "I can manage."

Morningleaf bit her lip. "I'm sorry." She liked Shadepebble and wanted to stay friends with her. "I was just trying to help, make it easier for you."

Shadepebble relaxed. "It's okay; I probably should draft, but I'd rather talk."

Morningleaf nickered. "Me too."

The two fillies flew in awkward silence—both strangers, but connected now on their journey. Shadepebble spoke first. "The black foal is your milk brother, right? You two nursed together?"

Surprise flickered through Morningleaf. She'd never

thought of Star in those terms. "Yes, we did."

"I remember when he was born," Shadepebble continued. "A messenger came from your herd to tell us the black foal had survived and was nursing off a surrogate mother. That was Silvercloud, right?"

Morningleaf was curious to hear the story retold by a foreign steed. "It was, and she's Silverlake now. She forced my birth early so she'd have milk for Star."

"That was risky," said Shadepebble.

Morningleaf nodded, and dipped under a wispy cloud so she wouldn't get wet. "Yes, but it was worth it, and I was born healthy."

"What was it like to grow up with him?"

"It wasn't easy," said Morningleaf with a sharp glance at Brackentail, who flew just ahead of them. "The herd was afraid of him."

"We used to pretend he was born to our herd," said Shadepebble.

"You did?" Morningleaf was astonished.

"Yes. I always played Star because I couldn't fly either, not at first."

"What was the game?" asked Morningleaf.

Shadepebble blinked, thinking. "Well, it was always a little different. I chased the other foals and they ran from me, pretending to be afraid. Anyone I caught was out of the game. Then we'd pretend it was my birthday and . . ." Shadepebble's voice faded.

"What?" pressed Morningleaf.

"It was a horrible game. Never mind." Shadepebble stared straight ahead. "We were just weanlings."

Morningleaf sighed. She could guess how the rest of the game went—they pretended to execute Star.

They coasted across a cluster of foothills and then dropped to an altitude where it was less windy. Shadepebble broke the silence. "Did Star choose to be the healer, or did the Hundred Year Star choose?"

Morningleaf hesitated, remembering the day Star healed Brackentail. He'd been overcome by anger, and she'd feared he would kill the colt. She believed Star was both healer and destroyer, but Morningleaf would not admit that out loud. Silverlake had told her before Star ever received his power that Morningleaf's purpose was to remind Star of who he was, and who he could be. Star could never know she'd doubted him, even for a second. It would break his heart. She answered simply. "He chose."

"So that means Nightwing chose to be bad," Shadepebble surmised in a whisper.

Morningleaf considered her point. "I suppose he did."

The fillies glided through the developing afternoon fog, absorbed by their thoughts.

Shivering and wet, Frostfire called the order to land. Morningleaf angled her wings and dropped out of the mist. She was delighted to see dark-green grass. They were out of the Ice Lands, and only patches of dirty snow remained. She landed and shook the dew off her feathers. It was windy, and within seconds she was shivering. "I wish Star were here," she said. Her flaxen mane was stuck flat on either side of her neck, drenched. "He could warm us."

Shadepebble nickered between clenched teeth. "That would be nice."

Frostfire interrupted them. "We'll sleep here tonight." The terrain was flat, and the pegasi could see for miles in each direction. Several trees dotted the grassy field, but not enough to obscure their view. Predators would not be able to approach them unseen, and the green grass was sweet. Morningleaf agreed it was a good place to rest.

Since there were no trees to block the wind, the pegasi huddled in small groups. Brackentail joined Morningleaf and Shadepebble.

"I miss my mother," confessed the Mountain Herd filly. "I didn't realize it while I was gone, but now that I'm close to home, I can't wait to see her."

Morningleaf nodded, overcome by her own loneliness. Only Brackentail was familiar to her. She barely knew Iceriver and the other three River Herd stallions, but she'd grown up with Brackentail. In a moment of homesickness, she nuzzled him and he startled, rocking backward on his hooves. "Sorry," she said, moving away from him.

He shook his head. "No, don't be." His eyes were large and sad, and Morningleaf softened toward him. Brackentail was more alone than any of them. His mother, Rowanwood, had not forgiven him for betraying Sun Herd. His old friends wouldn't speak to him, and Echofrost hated him. Morningleaf, Star, and Bumblewind were the only friends he had left. It was hard to believe.

Frostfire organized night sentries while Morningleaf, Shadepebble, and Brackentail grazed, filling their empty bellies. The sun burst through the clouds right before sunset. They each opened their wings to soak in as much heat as they could before nightfall. Morningleaf noticed that Shadepebble looked short and furry next to her own thin, sleek body. Back home, in Sun Herd's lands, she and Echofrost had made fun of Mountain Herd steeds, calling them mountain goats. Now she felt sorry for saying those things.

The pegasi settled head to tail for the night and were soon asleep, surrounded by Morningleaf's bodyguards.

Several hours later, Morningleaf woke to the frightful sounds of stallions screaming. "What's happening?" she squealed, and then she heard the sickening crunch of hoof against bone.

"Fly, Morningleaf!" whinnied Shadepebble. "Now!"

Morningleaf bolted blindly, flying toward the night stars, fear shaking her to her core.

24

ATTACK

"STOP HER!" ORDERED FROSTFIRE, POINTING AT Morningleaf. When the filly had agreed to let him escort her, he had begun to form a plan in his mind of how to dispose of her guards and kidnap her. And as they slept, he put his plan into effect. He had one of Morningleaf's guards pinned to the ground, having attacked him in his sleep, but his prize was slipping away.

His sky herder, Larksong, reared, her eyes gleaming, and she tore after the little chestnut. She caught Morningleaf fast and wrangled her back to land, clicking and whistling in the secret language of the sky herders, a tongue that had been passed down for generations, from one sky herder to the next.

Morningleaf's chest heaved, and her bright eyes spun wildly. "What are you doing?" she cried. Frostfire watched Shadepebble rush to her side, and the two fillies stood trembling.

Frostfire split the skull of the River Herd stallion lying on the ground and moved on to the next. Two of his warriors battled Iceriver. His sire's size and experience made up for his older age. Frostfire averted his eyes, unable to watch his father fight for his life.

Suddenly, a yearling stallion burst into view and rammed Frostfire—Brackentail.

"No, Brackentail! Fly away!" Morningleaf whinnied to her friend. "Get help. Get Star!"

Frostfire whirled and reared as Brackentail sank his teeth into his blue feathers. Brackentail reared too and struck Frostfire's chest with his front legs. Trails of blood rolled down Frostfire's hide, startling him. This ragged yearling had sharpened his hooves like a warrior!

Enraged, Frostfire snatched Brackentail by the mane and tossed him across the grass. Brackentail rolled onto his hooves and galloped back, charging Frostfire again. "You don't learn, do you," snapped Frostfire. He struck Brackentail's head with his hoof, knocking the yearling senseless, and Brackentail collapsed onto the grass.

"Stop this," squealed Shadepebble, fluttering her wings at Frostfire. "You promised to escort them. How could you go back on your word?"

Frostfire ignored his young aunt as a second River Herd stallion charged him and knocked him off his hooves. Frostfire fell and then rolled into the pinto's legs, collapsing him and slamming the warrior onto his side. Frostfire bit into his purple feathers and dragged him close. He arched his neck around the stallion's head and bit his throat. The pinto's eyes quickly emptied of life.

Frostfire hopped to his hooves and surveyed the battle. Iceriver and the rest of Morningleaf's protectors were down, except for one. Due to the advantage of the surprise attack, Frostfire's team was mostly unharmed, except that one of his warriors limped terribly, his leg hanging at an odd angle.

Just then the last of Morningleaf's guards, a palomino stallion, galloped past, chased by Larksong. Frostfire joined her and they circled him, forcing him to halt. He was young, maybe three or four years old, and his violet flight feathers were torn to shreds. Frostfire sneered and flashed his sharp incisors at the stallion. Larksong snatched the youngster's wings and held him in place as Frostfire approached.

The young River Herd stallion tried to hide his face,

but Frostfire saw the tears in his eyes, and this enraged him. "You failed your duties, warrior," Frostfire said to him. "Death is your only friend now."

"No! Let him go," cried Morningleaf. The young stallion wasn't much older than she.

The palomino glanced wildly at Frostfire, then he struggled to his hooves and leaned toward him, ears pinned. "*You* failed," he snapped. "You promised to hide Morningleaf."

Frostfire sidestepped the young warrior. "I *am* going to hide her," he said, "from Star."

Morningleaf gasped.

Frostfire shoved the young warrior hard enough to knock him flat on the grass, then he reared for the death-blow.

Morningleaf shook uncontrollably, her large amber eyes rimmed in white, her tail tucked, and her breaths coming in short huffs. "What's your name?" she whinnied to the fallen stallion. "I will tell all of River Herd about your bravery."

The light in the stallion's eyes blazed, and he spoke with deep pride. "I am Summerwind, colt of Raintree and Poppyfeather of Sun Herd, warrior of River Herd, and follower of Starwing."

Frostfire inhaled—*Starwing*! So River Herd considered

the black foal their over-stallion. Rockwing had been correct. The ridiculous council of pegasi was a ruse, and Frostfire had fallen for it. Star was their true leader. Frostfire grimaced. "Good-bye, Summerwind." Frostfire dropped his hoof and ended the young stallion's life.

"Frostfire!" Shadepebble stared at him, mouth gaping.

He bristled. "*This* is how we treat our enemies, Shadepebble."

Frostfire trotted to his sire, Iceriver, who was lying unconscious on the ground. He'd asked his team not to kill him, and they had followed his orders. He and his sire had spoken, but only a little on the journey, both feeling awkward. What Frostfire wanted to know, he hadn't mustered the courage to ask. He wondered why his father hadn't stood up to Petalcloud and kept him? But he also realized the answer didn't matter. Iceriver hadn't done it, and nothing could change that.

But Frostfire learned some things from his sire that he wished he had not. Namely that Frostfire's half sister, Lightfeather, was Star's dam. The news had crushed and overwhelmed Frostfire. He and Star were related by blood! And his sister's weakness revolted him. Lightfeather should have killed her colt when he was born. She was as useless as her sire. Frostfire wondered how many steeds in Anok knew he was Star's uncle? The messengers who proclaimed Star's birth had not named his dead mother—only the guardian herd. Frostfire hoped his shame would remain buried with his half sister forever.

Frostfire's injuries throbbed. He looked down and noticed smeared blood all over his chest. The smell would draw the wolves that lived in the area. His team also had bleeding wounds. He left Iceriver and gave orders to two of his stallions. "We need to clean up, fast. Go find a lake and then come back for us." They obeyed and kicked off, disappearing into the dark sky.

Frostfire glanced at his unconscious sire and fresh bitterness constricted his throat. He'd grown up without a proper dam or sire, a stranger in a strange herd. And Rockwing had pushed him harder than the other stallions, expecting more of him because of his large size and natural agility. Frostfire had graduated flight school early, entered the army as a two-year-old, and become the youngest captain in Mountain Herd's history. The other stallions had bullied him, until he earned their respect. Frostfire had to be crueler and meaner than all of them. But he'd done it.

He now stared at his true sire, torn between killing him and letting him live. Finally he let out his breath. He couldn't kill Iceriver. No matter what, he couldn't cross that line. "Break his wings," he ordered Larksong, who stood next to him.

Shadepebble lashed her tail. "That's your sire, Frostfire."

Frostfire reared, threatening to strike her, but he held back his deadly hooves. "It's why I'm not killing him," he rasped. "But I can't risk him following us."

Larksong interrupted. "You don't have to break his wings," she offered. "I could pull out his flight feathers."

He lashed his tail, impatient. "I'm not trained to do that. I don't know which ones to pull."

Frostfire, and all warriors, learned how to ground pegasi by making clean breaks in minor wing bones and to leave the roots untouched. Under proper care, the wings would heal and the steed would fly again. It was how they handled enemies they merely wanted to subdue, like during certain kidnappings or raids, but these operations were always quick, leaving no time for feather plucking.

"Sky herders are trained," said Larksong, flicking her tail. "It's gentler than breaking the wings but just as effective. He won't be able to fly. I'll do it."

"You're sure it'll work?" asked Frostfire, skeptical.

Larksong nodded, her eyes gleaming. "Every time."

"Do it then," ordered Frostfire. As she set to work, Frostfire noticed he'd lost track of Brackentail. The yearling was nowhere in sight. "Where's Brackentail?"

Morningleaf snorted, looking smug. "He's gone. You lost him."

Frostfire pinned his ears. "Hurry up," he snapped at the mares. "We have to get moving."

Shadepebble sat on her haunches, dazed. "Why have you done this, Frostfire?"

Frostfire was getting tired of being questioned, so instead of answering her, he pointed south. "See that lone oak tree?"

She nodded.

"That's our border. Cross it and go home. You too," he said to the stallion with the broken leg.

"I'm finished," said Larksong, spitting downy blue plumage from her mouth.

Frostfire turned to his group. "Good. Move out."

Morningleaf bolted, but Larksong snatched her quickly in a python-tight grip. Then two of his stallions took over and lifted Morningleaf by the bases of her wings.

"Where are you taking her?" asked Shadepebble, her expression fearful and perplexed. "You were supposed to hide her with her protectors. What are you up to?"

"Go *home*," answered Frostfire, seething.

"But what will I tell Rockwing? Your mission was to find me; he'll expect you home."

Frostfire was grim. "My mission was also to kidnap Morningleaf."

"So my sire knows about this?" Shadepebble asked, looking betrayed.

"Yes. And your kidnapping made the perfect excuse to go hunting for Morningleaf."

"But why do you want her?"

Frostfire glanced at Morningleaf, who was trembling. "Because Rockwing is going to take Star's birthland, and she's our hostage," he explained. "You know our herd is starving to death. Now fly home, Shadepebble, and don't worry about it or I'll tell Rockwing that you tried to join River Herd."

Shadepebble clenched her jaws and folded her wings, her fury pulsing in her veins.

Frostfire's scouts returned. "We found water, sir."

"Good." Frostfire turned to Shadepebble and the stallion with the broken leg. "Home is due south. Tell Rockwing I've succeeded in capturing Morningleaf, and I've left to hide her from Star."

Frostfire kicked off, his team trailing behind him. His

heart soared as he rose in altitude. He'd succeeded in both of his missions! He glanced back, taking stock of his team. Their numbers had been greatly reduced since he'd first set off from his territory. His original team of eight steeds had dwindled down to three—but they had Morningleaf!

Frostfire still couldn't believe Star had delivered the filly directly into his wings. And while he'd had to kill three River Herd stallions and ground his own sire, it was still a simpler operation than trying to steal her from Star.

Frostfire's remaining two stallions carried Morningleaf between them by the roots of her wings. The aqua-feathered filly was silent, and Frostfire was glad for that, but her expression was as sour as Shadepebble's had been. She was small for a Sun Herd steed but colorful, as most of them were. Her shiny coat lay flat and smooth. Her wings sparkled even in the moonlight. She returned his gaze. He expected to see anger or fear in her eyes—but he saw neither. He saw pity.

Frostfire scanned the ground for Brackentail but saw no sign of him. By the time the yearling alerted Star to the kidnapping, Frostfire would be long gone with his prize—and where he was taking Morningleaf, few steeds, if any, in Anok would think to look.

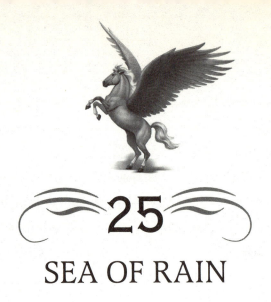

25

SEA OF RAIN

MANY DAYS PASSED, BUT IT WAS ALL A BLUR TO Morningleaf. She was exhausted. Frostfire flew them night and day. They stopped to graze and drink, but he refused to let them sleep longer than an hour. After a while he allowed her to fly on her own, and she plotted her escape, but no opportunities arose.

"There's a lake," whinnied the wiry buckskin mare, Larksong, raising her voice over the sweeping currents.

Frostfire flew straight ahead, not looking at it. "We just drank."

"I don't want a drink; I want a bath."

Morningleaf also wanted a bath. Dried sweat had curled her fur, her feathers were oily, and dead bugs decorated her mane and tail. It was the same with the others, and they stank, making them attractive to predators when they landed.

"Keep flying," said Frostfire.

Larksong groaned but did as she was told.

Morningleaf flew with a stallion at each flank, and scanned the scenery below, memorizing every detail of their route.

At dusk she caught sight of the southern end of the continent as they coasted toward it. Larksong saw it at the same time.

"Look! It's the Sea of Rain," the mare whinnied.

Frostfire cruised in a large descending circle before landing them on a white sand beach. When Morningleaf's hooves touched the warm sand, her legs folded. She immediately rolled, scratching her bug-infested back. Larksong joined her, keeping a sharp eye on her too.

Morningleaf stretched her wings and dug her shoulder blades into the blazing sand, letting the heat soak into her aching muscles and bones. *Was this the pain Star had felt most of his life,* she wondered, *this dull but persistent agony in the very center of her back?* The warm grains soothed the throbbing, and Morningleaf rested for several minutes with her legs straight up in the air, trying her best to relax. She yawned, stretching her clenched jaws for the first time in days, but tiny bugs biting at her flesh soon disrupted her peace.

Morningleaf rolled onto her side and gazed at the transparent green water, transfixed by the gentle lapping of the waves and the memories they evoked. Star had said that saltwater killed bugs and cleaned feathers better than lake water. He'd learned this while living in his cave with Crabwing. He'd also warned her about the dangerous whales and sharks that lived in the ocean. Morningleaf glanced at the clear water and, seeing nothing alarming, decided to take her chances. She trotted into the surf, followed by Frostfire's steeds.

A pod of dolphins played in the fading light. Their clicks and squeals resembled the unique language of the sky-herding mares. Farther out, Morningleaf sighted a coral reef alive with wiggling, nibbling fish, swaying plants, and skittering crabs. Morningleaf swiveled her ears, holding still and letting the gentle waves splash against her chest.

Larksong had also entered the water, and she swam nearby. She whistled and clicked to the dolphins, nickering with delight when they answered her. The dolphins darted in and out of the breakers, surfing toward shore, unafraid of the pegasi. Larksong flew out of the water and tried to herd them, but the sleek gray creatures slipped beneath the surface and disappeared. Larksong landed and shook herself. "Those dolphins are fast," she squealed, speaking to Frostfire.

The grumpy captain with one blue eye snorted, not interested in her fun. "We'll rest here tonight," he said.

Morningleaf trotted out of the waves and curled onto the beach to preen her feathers. She watched her captors closely, wanting to be ready if the chance to escape them arose.

"What do you think Nightwing will do when he returns to Anok?" Larksong asked Frostfire.

The white stallion glared at her. "What would *you* do if you were the most powerful pegasus in all the herds?"

"I would kill the over-stallions and take over their territories. There would be no more war and no more starvation. My herd would enjoy all of Anok instead of being stuck in one place."

"That sounds kind of nice," said one of the warriors.

Frostfire whinnied. "Not if you're an over-stallion! When Nightwing lived four hundred years ago, the herds lost their territories and were forced to live together. Those who opposed him were killed. He didn't allow them free range of Anok, or the freedom to rule themselves."

Morningleaf sighed and watched the surf roll and break, roll and break, as it had since the beginning of time. She wanted to speak but didn't dare. Freedom? It was an ideal pegasi fought hard to protect—an ideal that kept them prisoners of war.

Frostfire continued. "Maybe we'll get lucky, and Star and Nightwing will kill each other."

"How can you say that?" Morningleaf erupted. "You wanted Star dead! You all did! And now you expect him to risk his life to kill your enemy?" Her feathers rattled with fury. Of course Star *planned* to risk his life to save them, but they shouldn't expect it!

Her guards raced to control her, grabbing her wings as though she might fly away.

Frostfire bared his teeth. "You're wrong, filly. Rockwing never wanted Star dead. He tried to make a pact with him, but your black foal would not agree."

"Of course Star hadn't agreed," snapped Morningleaf. "Why would he ever agree to a pact with a cruel over-stallion like Rockwing?" She nestled back into the sand, deciding to save her strength. She had to escape. She had to return to Star. He didn't know what had happened to her—that she was in danger—unless Brackentail or

Iceriver had made it back to River Herd and told him. She snorted quietly at the thought of Brackentail and Star coming to her rescue, together.

The stallions spent the rest of the evening grazing near Morningleaf, never taking their eyes off her.

She fussed over the coastal plants, ripping into their roots and trying not to swallow any sand. She slept in fits and starts, plagued by nightmares of a black stallion smothering her in her sleep. She stared at the sky, wishing she could fly away, fly home. It was a very long night for her, and for the stallions who guarded her.

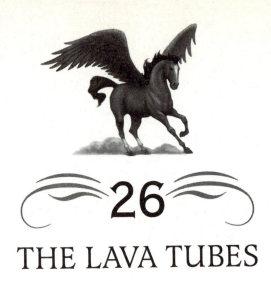

26

THE LAVA TUBES

MORNINGLEAF WAS GRATEFUL WHEN DAWN came and the brilliant sunrise split the darkness and bathed the rippling ocean in orange light.

Frostfire called for their attention and revealed his plan. "Today we'll cross the border into Jungle Herd's territory," he said. "We're going to hide Morningleaf in the lava tubes."

Morningleaf's gut clenched . . . *lava tubes*?

Larksong arched her neck. "The lava tubes are just a legend."

"No. They're real," insisted Frostfire. "But few pegasi outside of Jungle Herd know that, so Star won't look for Morningleaf there."

"But how do *you* know they're real?" asked Larksong.

Morningleaf ransacked her mind for stories or legends about the lava tubes. She remembered something about Jungle Herd yearlings daring each other to enter them, and then the steeds getting lost forever. The tubes were a maze, but it was believed that they had collapsed when the volcano erupted one thousand years earlier.

Frostfire answered Larksong. "When I flew the Veins as part of my training, I explored the other territories. Jungle Herd was nesting in the north, so I flew across their border into their southern territory. I wanted to see the birthland of Nightwing."

"Did you see the Valley of Tears?" asked Larksong.

"Yes, I saw everything: the nesting grounds where Nightwing was born, the Valley of Tears where Spiderwing attacked Moonwing's army, and the volcano they call Firemouth. The lava tubes have re-formed, but Star doesn't know about them, and neither does Nightwing. We'll be safe there."

"But what about Jungle Herd?" asked one of the warriors. "They'll kill us on sight."

"By now they've received the warning about Nightwing and left to hide in the Trap. Their territory should be empty."

Larksong opened her wings. "I can't wait to see the Valley of Tears," she said. "Spiderwing outsmarted an entire army by himself—and he was just a yearling."

Morningleaf wouldn't admit it out loud, but she was excited too. The legends of Anok had always fascinated her.

Frostfire gave the order to move out, and Morningleaf cantered across the sand with them. One by one they galloped into the sky, which was muggy but clear. The shoreline curved toward the southern tip of the continent, but they flew east, straight into Jungle Herd's territory.

"There's the Wing River," Frostfire said.

Morningleaf glanced down and saw a shimmering path of blue water. She followed it with her eyes until she spotted the lake that fed it. Her mother had taught her the topography of the other territories, so she knew the lake was called Crystal Lake.

She traced the water to where the Wing River forked, and her mind raced, exhilarated. The War of the Yearlings had been fought there. Morningleaf soaked up all history from the elders, but this battle was one of her favorites because Spiderwing and Moonwing were the youngest over-stallions in Anok's history—both yearlings. Next to Lightfeather and Raincloud, Spiderwing was her third favorite hero.

To Morningleaf's left was Firemouth, the massive and angry volcano that had been threatening Jungle Herd since it last erupted one thousand years ago. Smoke rose out of its neck, and lava dribbled down its sides like the hot yolk from a cracked bird's egg.

Frostfire landed his team at the base of this black mountain. The vegetation that was thick and damp in the flatlands melted away as the land tilted toward the mountain's smoldering peak.

"Stay close," Frostfire commanded. "Everything in this territory is dangerous, even the plants. The river water near the volcano is warm, but it's filtered by the mountain, so it's safe to drink." He pointed his wing at Crystal Lake. "But that water is not safe for drinking or swimming."

Morningleaf shuddered. She knew Crystal Lake was infested with fanged fish that could strip the flesh off a pegasi in seconds. It was said the bones of dead pegasi covered the bottom of the lake, and they re-formed at night to walk the land as a herd of skeletons.

Frostfire shivered in the warm breeze as though he were reading her mind. "Here's the entrance to the tubes," he said.

Morningleaf startled when Firemouth boomed and the land shook. She leaped sideways and huddled against a tree.

"No!" cried Frostfire. He knocked her away from the trunk, and she tumbled into a clump of hanging vines, becoming briefly entangled.

"What was that for?" she demanded.

He pointed at something in the tree. She squinted and then gasped. It was a fat yellow snake, longer than Star's wings.

"That constrictor is waiting for a fool like yourself to walk beneath it," said Frostfire. "Jaguars wait in trees too, and then they drop on you. Everything here is dangerous." He glared at her with his mismatched eyes. "Stay on the animal paths."

Morningleaf took a longer look at her surroundings and saw faint trails worn through the plants. She nodded her understanding.

Far above them, Firemouth belched, and fresh smoke and lava erupted from its neck. A putrid smell filled her nostrils.

"Get used to that," said Frostfire. "It's an active volcano."

Morningleaf watched the lava slowly freeze as it

traveled down the side of the mountain, halting halfway. The smoke curled into the clouds. "We'll be safe here?" she muttered to herself.

Frostfire guided Morningleaf and his team into the lava tube, which led toward the belly of the volcano. Their hoofbeats reverberated in the darkness and faded away. Morningleaf's hooves slipped on loose rocks. She looked down and saw that bright crystals littered the smooth floor. Above her, sharp lavacicles hung from the ceiling. The tubes themselves were round and even, as though they'd been carved into the rock by a thinking creature.

Frostfire's team walked deep into the tunnel, pushing Morningleaf ahead of them. She flared her nostrils, taking in unfamiliar and unpleasant scents. Her ears twisted, filtering the noises for anything dangerous. Several more tubes fanned out from the first. Some returned to the open jungle, and these tunnels brought in daylight and fresh air. The others drifted into darkness.

Frostfire threw a rock into a dark tunnel, and the noise of it echoed back to them for a long time. "This is a dangerous maze," he commented. "Don't go down the dark tubes. But this is the spot. This is where we'll hide her."

They had halted in a large chamber, which glowed from a mysterious light source. Morningleaf stared at the black tubes leading off the cavern. Perhaps in the utter darkness of them she would be able to escape. Her daring thoughts caused her heart to race and her feathers to molt off her wings. She noticed her captors watching her.

"Nothing to say?" jeered Larksong.

"Don't talk to her," scolded Frostfire.

But Morningleaf answered. "We should be fighting Nightwing, not each other."

Frostfire huffed. "This has nothing to do with Nightwing. We're taking Sun Herd's land, and by controlling you, we can control Star. He can't stop us."

"But he doesn't want that territory back," sputtered Morningleaf.

"He says that now," said Frostfire, "but just wait. He'll change when he grows up and begins to crave a territory of his own."

"He's not like you."

Frostfire snorted. "He's exactly like me."

She turned her back on Frostfire, too upset to continue arguing.

Frostfire snapped his team to attention. "This is our new home. Let's clean it and find food." He gave each steed a job. Two cut edible plants and grasses with their teeth and brought them into the tube for storage, Larksong picked fruit, and he made Morningleaf sweep the floor clean with her wings.

She worked tirelessly, grateful to be doing something. She cleaned the main chamber and avoided the long black tunnels. She swept the pretty crystals into one pile, because they made her feel better. She pushed the dirt and the bat droppings out and down the side of the volcano. Her feathers reeked of the guano and the mud caused by the water leaking down the smooth rock walls. She wanted to wash her wings but was too angry to ask permission. She let them hang at her sides, hoping the chance to clean them would come later. Sweating and tired, she suddenly began to sob.

Frostfire ignored her.

Once the tears came, they would not stop. Morningleaf curled into a ball and cried into her filthy feathers. She had tried to put Frostfire's attack out of her mind, but in the darkness it was as vivid as day. She heard the dying groans of the River Herd stallions in her mind. She saw Summerwind's handsome face, and Brackentail being thrown and knocked out. She saw Larksong yanking out Iceriver's feathers. Morningleaf sobbed until her tears ran out, then she lurched to her hooves.

She walked to the edge of the main tube, her appointed

guard following her, and looked out at the jungle. Huge, colorful birds flew over the broad-leafed trees. The afternoon air was stifling and smelled of rain. It was difficult to breathe. Monkeys screamed and scrambled up the branches, stopping often to groom each other or to squabble. Morningleaf took a deep breath and coughed.

Frostfire jerked his head toward her. "Are you sick?"

She blinked at him. "I don't think so."

"Stick out your tongue."

She did, reluctantly.

He tossed his mane. "You're fine, but if your throat starts to hurt, tell me."

"Are *you* sick?" she asked, suddenly horrified. *Was Frostfire carrying the plague?*

He turned his back on her and waited for Larksong to return, but he didn't answer her question, and that scared her. If someone on his team had the plague, she would never escape this place! She had to get away as soon as possible.

By evening they had supplies and soft bedding. Frostfire set up the night sentries and then stood at the end of a lava tube, staring at the sky. Larksong joined him, and Morningleaf heard her say, "Look! A shooting star."

Morningleaf closed her eyes, still overcome by sadness.

Up in the vastness of space, glittering stars died and fell, burning trails of starfire in their wakes. It happened all the time, but tonight the falling star felt like an omen for the pegasi of Anok, for they had fixed their hopes on a black stallion born of those very fragile stars.

27

ICERIVER

STAR GLIDED OFF THE HIGHEST PEAK OF THE HOOF-beat Mountains to a lower one that was more sheltered from the wind and rain. A half moon had passed since Morningleaf had left with Frostfire, and Star was sick with worry. Was Frostfire treating her well? Was she safe?

When Star wasn't fretting over Morningleaf, he was practicing with his starfire, burning trees and exploding boulders. Bumblewind tried to keep him company, but Star preferred the highest peaks of the Hoofbeat Mountains, and his friend couldn't breathe well there. So Star asked Bumblewind to watch over the Trap from the lower elevations while Star kept his eyes trained toward the west.

Spring had descended with a fury upon the north. Gnats and mosquitoes erupted with warmer weather, pestering the pegasi incessantly. Moose, elk, and caribou dropped their young and traveled in massive migrations, devouring the tundra as they passed through. The wolves howled each night after their successful hunts, and their pups suckled contentedly. Foxes and ground squirrels, birds and rabbits, bustled with an energy that was foreign to the same creatures living farther south. It was as though they knew spring would be short-lived and then summer, with its seeming unending daylight, would pass just as fast, and then the long winter would return and pursue them to the edge of their endurance.

Star fanned his wings to shelter himself from the rain that was falling, and he became captivated by a nest of baby birds on the downward slope of his peak. They were blind, with their mouths open, and they ate whatever their mother pushed into their throats. Later she would shove them out of the nest, one by one, and they would either fly or fall to their deaths. Star was daydreaming, remembering what it was like before he could fly, when Bumblewind whistled, alerting him that a herd was approaching.

Star leaped off his plateau, coasted through the pounding rain, and landed next to Bumblewind.

"It's Desert Herd," his friend informed him. "Look, there's Sandwing."

Star and Bumblewind trotted forward to greet the over-stallion of the soaking-wet and exhausted herd. Their climate was always hot, so their coats were thin, and so were they. Star was glad winter was over, for Desert Herd's sake. "Greetings," Star said, shaking the water off his hide.

The handsome palomino over-stallion was wary of Star, approaching slowly, but the threat of the Destroyer created an uneasy truce between them. "Any sign of Nightwing?" Sandwing asked.

"He's close." Star bristled at the thought of Nightwing. The heady force of the Destroyer curled around him like an invisible mist—cloying at his mind and tugging at him like a persistent foal. "Very close," he added.

Sandwing swiveled his ears, tracking all sounds in the area. Star noticed the differences between them. Since Desert Herd steeds kept their lineage pure, they weren't mixed with the heavier steeds of northern Anok. Sandwing was tall, thin, and bound with tight, flat muscles. He had an extra-deep chest for breathing in high altitudes where Desert Herd steeds liked to fly, and his hooves were extra hard to deal with the extreme heat of the desert floor. "A storm is coming," said Sandwing.

Star nodded. "I know."

"What does Nightwing want?" asked the over-stallion, clearly baffled by the threat he couldn't see.

Star tossed his sopping mane. "I don't know exactly, but I can feel him. His intentions aren't good."

"And you think hiding in there is going to save us?" Sandwing nodded toward the Trap.

Star followed his eyes. "It might."

Sandwing seemed to appreciate the harsh truth. "Not every steed from my herd came," he said.

Star flicked his ears. "What do you mean?"

"Many stayed behind. They won't leave our homeland."

Star dropped his head, sighing. "The same is true for Jungle Herd. They arrived yesterday, but not all of them, and not their over-stallion. He's hiding the rest deep in their territory, in the Cloud Forest. And Snow Herd has refused to hide altogether."

"That's good, isn't it? They're sick with the plague."

"We would have kept them quarantined," said Star. He didn't think it was good that Snow Herd wasn't coming. If the plague didn't wipe them out, Nightwing might; but they didn't want to owe Star, or River Herd, for anything.

Sandwing shrugged. "I understand. I almost didn't come myself."

"Why did you change your mind?"

"The newborns," said Sandwing, blinking raindrops out of his eyes. "They deserve a chance to grow up."

Star nodded, thoughtful.

Sandwing faced his herd, which numbered in the thousands. "Into the Trap," he ordered them. "Stay together and go in deep." His mingling herd instantly divided themselves into groups and marched into the trees in perfect, straight lines. Morningleaf knew a lot about the other herds from legends, and she'd told Star that Desert Herd had a fierce system of discipline and the best-trained army in Anok.

"I'll show you to your camp," offered Bumblewind. Silverlake had sectioned the Trap into five encampments, each complete with a water source, to help prevent the inevitable fighting that would break out in close quarters.

Sandwing trotted behind Bumblewind but said over his shoulder, "May the Ancestors be with you, Star."

Star had been watching the colorful lights migrate across the sky almost every evening, swirling over his head, and he could feel the love of his Ancestors beaming down on him. "They are," he said to the over-stallion.

Silverlake landed next to Star, startling him out of his thoughts. "You were right," she said. "I can't see the pegasi once they enter the forest, and the ceiling of leaves and branches is blocking most of the rain. It's comfortable in there, a good place to hide."

"Let's fly over it and see how it looks from above."

Silverlake nodded, and they kicked off and glided over the trees, which were lightly flecked in fast-melting snow. They saw no sign of Desert Herd from the air. "This is good," said Star.

But Silverlake had stopped listening. She narrowed her eyes. "Look there." Her gaze turned south. "Something is wrong."

Dewberry, who Silverlake had appointed to watch for predators and incoming herds, was flying fast over the Trap, her ears pinned and her neck flat. She looked alarmed. Star and Silverlake flew toward her, and they met over the trees, hovering in place.

"What is it?" Silverlake asked her.

"A lone stallion is coming this way. He's injured."

"A Desert Herd steed?" asked Silverlake.

"I don't think so, but I didn't stick around to find out," said Dewberry, breathing hard. "He needs help. Now."

"Show us where," whinnied Star.

Dewberry led Star and Silverlake away from the Trap. Thundersky galloped into the clouds to join them. "What's happening?" he asked. "Is it Nightwing?"

Silverlake answered. "No. It's an injured stallion, alone. He's coming this way."

Star followed them all to the flat, treeless tundra. Thick clouds blocked out the sun, so the intruding stallion was hard to see at first. Pale-blue feathers littered the trail behind him, and the stallion was dark silver. Star's heart sank. "It looks like Iceriver."

Silverlake gasped. "Oh no—he's supposed to be with Morningleaf!" She angled her wings and jetted forward. The rest followed.

Star's chest tightened as he flew closer. It *was* Iceriver. They landed, surrounding him. Iceriver's wings were missing all their flight feathers, and dried blood crusted the top of his head. His tongue hung from his mouth, devoid of color.

"What happened?" cried Silverlake.

Iceriver had aged many seasons in the short time he'd been gone. His muscles sagged, and his back had hollowed. The rain splattered his body, and he ignored it. His eyes looked dead already. "Frostfire," he said, wheezing. "He . . . took Morningleaf."

Star sucked in his breath, and his gut lightened like a leaf caught in the wind.

"Your own colt did this to you?" gasped Silverlake.

Iceriver nodded, groaning with pain.

"Where did he take her?" asked Thundersky, pawing the moss, his eyes murderous.

Iceriver shook his head. "They knocked me out. When I woke, my team was dead, and my flight feathers were gone. They flew away, leaving no hoofprints to tell me which way they went." He gagged on his dry tongue.

Star surged forward, his heart racing. "I'm going to heal you."

Iceriver shook his head. "No. I delivered my message. I'm done." His legs buckled and he fell.

"Get up," Thundersky ordered.

Iceriver grunted, and Star saw the clouds reflected in the stallion's eyes, drifting across them like misty spirits. "Please let me help you." Star's throat seized as he forced out the words. He felt sick. Iceriver was dying.

Iceriver took several deep breaths before he exhaled slowly and his body relaxed. "I see Lightfeather," he said, "and all my foals." He sank into the tundra moss with a peaceful expression on his face, and his vacant eyes remained open. Iceriver was gone.

Silverlake burst into tears.

Star stared at Iceriver, stunned at his final words. He was with Lightfeather, Star's mother, and he was happy to see her. Star had never bonded with Iceriver, who was his grandsire, maybe because Iceriver had let his mate Petalcloud chase Lightfeather out of Snow Herd, but now Star had lost his chance to know his grandsire better.

Star exhaled and let go of his feelings. It was too late, and Morningleaf was in danger.

Thundersky spoke softly. "Fly straight and find your rest, Iceriver, born of Snow Herd, council member of River Herd, and sire of Lightfeather."

After a long moment of silence, with only the sound of the rain between them, Dewberry spoke quietly but firmly. "We have to sink his body in Pebble Lake," she said, referring to the large pond they'd named after Shadepebble, who'd almost drowned in it.

Star and the others stared at her as though she'd gone mad.

She explained. "We can't make a grave—Nightwing will see it and know that pegasi live near. If we're hiding the living, shouldn't we also hide the dead?"

"Dewberry makes sense," said Thundersky.

"We drink that water," said Silverlake, always the practical one.

"There's another over there." Dewberry pointed east.

"All right," said Thundersky, his voice ragged with grief for Iceriver. "Please gather some stallions, Dewberry, and take care of Iceriver. There's no time for a ceremony; we have a greater concern to attend to: Morningleaf is Frostfire's captive."

"Right away," said Dewberry, and she left to get help.

Silverlake paced, trampling the muddy soil. "Why would Frostfire kill Morningleaf's protectors and take her like that? We saved Shadepebble."

"He lied to us, and he broke his promise," said Thundersky, shaking his head as though he should have known.

"But why?" Silverlake repeated.

"Maybe Rockwing is behind this. He used Morningleaf once before," Thundersky reminded her, "to trade her for Star."

"Of course," said Silverlake. "But what does he want this time?" The cold afternoon breeze blew her soaking wet forelock into her eyes. She tossed the hair out of her way. "It must have been his plot all along. Frostfire wasn't looking for Shadepebble; he was looking for Morningleaf."

"Or he was looking for both," said Star. "And we

delivered them to him," Bitterness squeezed his throat.

Silverlake interrupted. "It's done. Let's just find her."

"We chose Frostfire so that I *wouldn't* be able to find her," said Star in agony. "Where do we start?"

Suddenly, orange feathers tumbled from the sky. Star looked up to see a lone figure. It landed in front of them just as lightning rattled the darkening sky. It was Brackentail! Star tensed, his gut clenching. Had the Betrayer betrayed them again?

28

RETURNING HOME

BRACKENTAIL LANDED, OUT OF BREATH.

"Why aren't you with Morningleaf?" Star brayed.

With heaving sides, he sputtered. "Frostfire attacked the stallions. I fought him, I tried . . . but Morningleaf screamed at me to get you." He glanced at Star and began to cry.

"You didn't follow her!" whinnied Star.

"What could I do?" he asked, wiping his eyes. "Free her from Frostfire by myself? I came to get help." He dropped his head. "I'm sorry."

Star flinched when a clap of thunder shocked his ears. Heavy raindrops began pouring from the clouds, drenching all of them.

"Did you help Frostfire take Morningleaf?" snapped Thundersky, flashing his old anger at Brackentail for betraying Sun Herd and pressing into him with his chest.

"No, sir!" Brackentail whinnied, and his devastated expression told Star his words were true.

"Where did they take her?" asked Silverlake, more gently than her mate.

"When I saw the fight was lost, I ran and hid in the woods," said Brackentail, trembling. "Frostfire sent Shadepebble home, telling her that stealing Morningleaf had been part of his mission all along."

"So Rockwing *is* behind this," said Silverlake.

Star pranced in an anxious circle, crushing the lichen and stirring up the dirt, which quickly turned to mud in the rain. "This is my fault. I asked her to go." Lightning sizzled toward land and struck, not far from where Star stood. He felt his world spinning out of control. He couldn't breathe, or think.

Bumblewind had finished with the Desert Herd steeds and he fluttered from the sky, landing next to Star. His eyes rounded when he saw Brackentail. "You all need to get out of here before someone gets struck by lightning." His voice was drowned out by more thunder.

Silverlake ignored him and neighed over the explosive

sky to Brackentail. "But why does Rockwing want Morningleaf?"

"Rockwing wants Star's homeland," explained Brackentail. "He's holding Morningleaf hostage to get it." Lightning burst over their heads, and Brackentail's legs sprawled in fear.

Star cocked his head, squinting against a sudden blast of wind. "But I haven't claimed the territory."

"I think I understand," snorted Thundersky, turning to Star. "Rockwing doesn't believe you'll let him have it. Your mother is buried there. It's sacred ground to you, and it's where you were born. You're still young, Star, and you don't know how your feelings will change when you grow into a stallion, a powerful stallion. You'll want to settle someday, and you'll be able to take any land you want— why not your own homeland? That's what Rockwing's afraid of, and he's stolen Morningleaf to control you."

"Yes, Thundersky is right," said Brackentail.

Star's spinning world crashed around him, and he became oblivious to the storm that had descended upon them like Brackentail's bad news—quick and terrifying, and out of their control. "Morningleaf is a hostage, again," whispered Star. "Because of me."

Silverlake's breathing quickened. "Not again! Not if I

can help it." Star saw the determination in her eyes. Silverlake was no longer lead mare, so she was free to leave her herd and risk everything for the sake of her filly. "Let's go find her!"

"Wait," whinnied Brackentail, holding up his orange-feathered wing. "I'm not finished." He shook his soaking neck and continued. "After Frostfire left, the strangest thing happened." He looked at each of them. "Shadepebble returned and found me. She was alone."

The steeds blinked at him, unimpressed. "So? Why is that important?" asked Bumblewind.

Brackentail explained. "She was so upset by Frostfire's betrayal, she decided to help us. Don't you see? Rockwing's filly is on our side."

Lightning struck a nearby tree, and the trunk cracked in half and tumbled onto its side. The pegasi spooked, scattering and then regrouping.

Bumblewind gulped and prodded Star. "We have to get out of here."

"But Shadepebble's just a yearling, and a runt at that," said Thundersky, also ignoring Bumblewind. "What can she do?"

Brackentail pricked his ears. "Rockwing has our filly, and now we have his. Don't you see?"

"What are you suggesting, Brackentail?" said

Silverlake, flattening her ears. Another burst of lightning crackled down from the sky, blinding the pegasi.

"We have to seek shelter—NOW!" whinnied Bumblewind. They all galloped away but neighed to one another over the beating of their hooves.

"It's Shadepebble's idea," Brackentail explained, running with one eye on the thundering sky. "She'll pretend to be our captive, to give us leverage against her sire, Rockwing."

Silverlake blinked. "That's incredible. Where is she?"

Thunder rumbled hard and violent, assaulting their sensitive ears.

"I sent her ahead, to the Sun Herd lands to find Hazelwind and his group. They must still be there since they haven't arrived yet to hide in the Trap, but they're in great danger. Frostfire already sent messengers to Rockwing that he'd captured Morningleaf. That's all Rockwing was waiting for. He will march on Sun Herd's territory and claim it immediately. Rockwing's army will destroy Hazelwind and his followers. Hazelwind can use Shadepebble as a hostage, to stop the attack. Surely Rockwing will want to save his last remaining filly."

Thundersky huffed. "That was smart thinking, Brackentail."

Silverlake neighed over the wind and rain. "So where

is Morningleaf? With Rockwing?"

Brackentail shook his head. "No. Frostfire is hiding her far away, and he didn't say where, but I think we could use Shadepebble to get her back too. She's willing to help us."

Thundersky glanced at the storm, which was gaining in power. "Let's go to the Sun Herd territory then," he said, pinning his ears. "I want to be there when Rockwing arrives. I'll make him find Frostfire and return my filly."

All the pegasi listening flared their wings and rattled their feathers.

"I'm ready," said Star. He kicked off, not caring who followed him, just anxious to go. But then everything suddenly turned black, and he smashed into a tree.

"Star!"

Splitting pain seared his mind. He gripped his head in his wings and stumbled across the tundra. He vaguely heard his friends trotting after him. Pain stabbed his brain like a bird was pecking at it. He ducked with each blow, moaning.

Star collapsed, and his body convulsed. He heard Silverlake scream his name, then the forest blurred and disappeared.

Star was flying fast over the ocean. The sudden shift

made him dizzy. This was another vision. A pegasus flew beside him, and Star saw black feathers. He didn't have to turn his head to know it was Nightwing. "Leave me alone," Star neighed.

Star's headache subsided, and he tried to get his bearings. They were flying over the Great Sea, he guessed. He looked down and saw blue sharks following them, snapping at their hooves. He tucked his legs up tight.

"Why am I here with you?" Star asked. "Why won't you leave me alone?"

"Look ahead," said the Destroyer.

Star looked and faltered, almost tumbling into the sea. A short distance away was the western coast of Anok. Star recognized his old cave and Crabwing's Bay. Nightwing soared toward it, and Star realized the Destroyer would make landfall today!

Star floundered to get ahead, to fly faster and warn his friends. Then the world went black again and he fell. When he opened his eyes, he was upside down in the mud, his legs galloping in the air. Silverlake fanned his face with her wings. "Star?" she said.

He focused and stood up.

"What did you see?" she asked, her voice trembling.

"It's Nightwing. He's almost to our coast."

His friends stared at him, stunned. "We're out of time," said Silverlake. She glanced at her mate. "We have to warn Hazelwind."

Bumblewind peered at the clouds sizzling with electricity. "We shouldn't fly during a lightning storm."

"We have to," cried Silverlake.

"Fly low and fast," said Thundersky, and Star had never seen him looking so concerned.

Star turned to Brackentail. "Go back and warn the herds in the Trap. Tell them they must not fly the skies any longer. It's all come down to this. They must hide so Nightwing doesn't see them. Will you do that?"

"Of course," Brackentail said, looking exhausted.

Star kicked off and the others followed; they didn't waste time with good-byes. They flew just below the black clouds.

"Where is Nightwing now?" Silverlake asked Star.

"Not far," he said, feeling sicker. Iceriver was dead, Morningleaf was kidnapped, the plague-ridden Snow Herd steeds had refused to hide, Rockwing was heading toward Hazelwind, and Nightwing was about to make landfall in Anok. It was overwhelming.

Star shouldered the cold breeze as Silverlake, Thundersky, and Bumblewind drafted behind him. He had to learn how to block Nightwing out of his mind. As long as the stallion could track him and invade him like he'd just done, everyone around Star was in danger.

They flew steadily for a few hours, dodging bolts of lightning, and with each passing mile, Star grew more anxious. Finally he spoke, "I can fly much faster than this on my own."

Silverlake nickered, unsurprised. "Go ahead, Star. We'll meet you there."

Star nodded and pushed down on the wind with his wings. He rocketed up and out of the storm, climbing until he could see the curve of the planet. The winds buffeted him at speeds that ripped loose his feathers. Star rounded his wings, gripped the current, and set his course for Sun Herd's territory, his birth land.

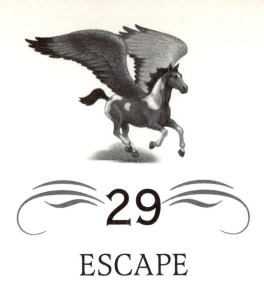

29

ESCAPE

A SHADOW OF WINGS DARKENED THE SIDE OF THE
volcano where Frostfire had led his group to drink from
the steamy river. "Inside," ordered Frostfire in a hushed
whinny.

Larksong and the others scooted back into the lava
tubes.

"It's a Jungle Herd patrol," commented Frostfire. "It
looks like some of their steeds decided not to hide in the
Trap."

Several days had passed, and Frostfire kept his pegasi
inside the cave except to drink. The tubes were miserable—
hot and dark. They unraveled through the belly of the
volcano for miles. Twice already his steeds had gotten

lost. Strange noises echoed from the depths, and his team was certain dangerous creatures lurked there. Frostfire insisted it was only rats, but that did little to relax them.

Frostfire waited until the Jungle Herd patrol was well out of sight, then he sent the two stallions to gather coconuts. His team liked the taste of the sweet milk inside, and besides, his steeds were bored. Cracking the coconuts would entertain them.

Just after the stallions left, the rain began to fall. Frostfire sighed. It rained every afternoon here for hours. He and his pegasi stood at the mouth of the tube looking out, waiting. Waiting for the rain to stop, waiting for Nightwing to come, waiting for Star to defeat him, and waiting for Rockwing to make his exchange: Morningleaf for Sun Herd's territory. The waiting set Frostfire's feathers on edge.

When the stallions returned, they dropped the coconuts on the rock floor of the tubes and watched them roll. "Who wants to play wing toss?" asked Larksong.

Frostfire glowered at her, but the others leaped at the chance to play, to do something.

"Can we?" she asked him, fluttering her long black lashes.

Frostfire nodded. He hated his inability to say no to

her, and he hated the fact that she knew he couldn't say no to her. Frostfire left a gray pinto stallion in charge of Morningleaf and flew to watch the game.

Since there were three of them, Frostfire and his warrior stallion teamed up against Larksong. They tossed the coconuts back and forth between them. After each catch, they stepped back a winglength. As they drew apart, the game became more challenging. The first steed to miss a catch was out, and then the second, leaving the last steed the winner.

They played several rounds before dusk fell and Frostfire grew nervous. "I'm going to check on Morningleaf." He abandoned the game and trotted back to the lava tubes. The pinto stallion and Morningleaf were dozing side by side. Frostfire relaxed and joined them, standing just inside the dark maw of the tunnel as he watched the warm rain drip off the broad jungle leaves.

Moments later, a sharp squeal jolted Frostfire out of his thoughts. The pinto stallion slammed into him, knocking Frostfire and Morningleaf sideways, but the stallion wasn't looking at them. He was staring fearfully into the blackness behind them.

"Watch it!" Frostfire scolded.

The pinto ignored him, and was soon bucking and

flapping his wings. Morningleaf skittered across the rocks, trying to avoid being crushed by the thrashing pegasus. Frostfire looked closer and saw blood dripping down the pinto's white-and-gray back. "What's happening to you?" he asked.

The stallion trotted frantically in a tight circle, his lips curled, his chest heaving. He wasn't listening to Frostfire; he was snapping his jaws and twisting his ears. Frostfire and Morningleaf scrambled farther out of his way. Something had attacked him.

Frostfire reared, trying to see over the pinto's back. Then a flurry of wings burst into the cavern, and supersonic whistles confused Frostfire's ears as the stallion's attackers swarmed: bats! They swirled out of the black depths and landed on the pegasi, biting their necks.

Frostfire trumpeted a warning to the steeds outside, all the while flapping his wings, hitting bats, and smashing them against the rock walls. The chestnut filly was also under attack. Frostfire was overwhelmed by twin white fangs, transparent wings, and tiny, clawed feet. Bats charged him with their mouths open, slicing and biting him all over. Frostfire neighed in frustration. He bucked and they flew off him, but returned with a fury. A big one landed on his neck. Frostfire felt the sharp poke of its fangs piercing his hide. He squealed with anger.

This was not an enemy he could effectively fight in a small space. "Out of the cave!" Frostfire whinnied. He flew out of the tube into the fresh air. The bats followed him and then disappeared into the jungle, but Frostfire still heard their awful squeaks.

He shook himself, while his pinto stallion rolled in the damp grass. The rest of the steeds landed next to him. "What happened?" asked Larksong.

"Bats," said Frostfire.

Larksong inspected his wounds and then stiffened. "Where's Morningleaf?"

Frostfire glanced around but didn't see her. He neighed, furious, and flew back into the tube. He and his team searched all the areas they'd been exploring over the last few days. They were empty.

Morningleaf was gone.

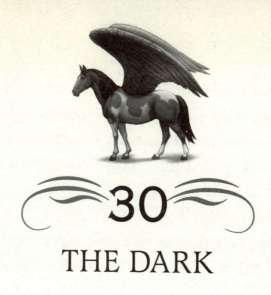

30

THE DARK

WHEN THE BATS ATTACKED, MORNINGLEAF seized her chance to escape. She slipped into one of the dark lava tubes and crept as quickly as she could into the blackness. Behind her she heard squealing and the fluttering of wings—bat wings and pegasi wings—as the horde of fanged fliers snacked on the stallions. She'd only suffered a few bites herself before she darted away. Ahead of her, the sounds echoed against the solid silence of stone.

Morningleaf felt her way through the tubes using her sensitive wingtips. She swallowed the urge to trot, fearing she'd fall into a hole and slide into the lava that she was sure ran in hot rivers under the mountain. As the whinnies of the stallions died away, she became aware of her rapid breathing, which filled the silence. Meanwhile the tube became narrower and tighter. Soon she bumped her head on the ceiling and had to lower her neck. Fear slithered through her gut like a tangle of snakes, and every instinct told her to turn back.

But Morningleaf kept going.

She had to warn Star. He had no idea Rockwing plotted against him. Memories of the fearless and arrogant over-stallion of Mountain Herd made her feel sick and angry, and those emotions—mixed with her fear of the dark—left her light-headed. Morningleaf halted and took a deep breath, her ears swiveling. She heard nothing but her own panting breath.

She continued forward with her neck low as the tube continued to shrink. "I'm going to get stuck," she whispered fearfully, and this caused her steady heartbeat to thrum, thin and fast.

Morningleaf could not return the way she had come—she'd be captured again—so she kept going, crouching now. Her brother, Hazelwind, was also in grave danger. He was living in Sun Herd's old lands with his followers. When Rockwing took over the territory, he would drive Hazelwind out . . . and poor Echofrost! The sight of Mountain Herd warriors flying over the Blue Mountains would fracture what was left of Echofrost's mind, she was sure of it. Morningleaf smacked into a wall. "Ouch." She froze, listening. Yes, there it was—the noise of hoofbeats and sharp whistles sounded from behind her. It was the sky-herding mare, Larksong, coming after her!

Morningleaf spread her wings, feeling the walls for an opening. Her best hope was to get deeply lost in the maze, or to get out quickly, while they still believed she was inside. A gentle breeze, like a caterpillar's breath, wafted through the tunnel and fluttered across her eyelashes. It was an air current! *I must be near an opening,* she thought. She followed it and found another tube, this one larger and to her left. She turned into it and after ten steps came to another tube. She turned again, losing the flutter of air. She paused, baffled.

Morningleaf turned in a slow circle, listening. The sounds of the mare were far away now. She hoped she was deep enough inside the volcano that Frostfire's team wouldn't find her. Besides, with every step she risked making noise, or tripping and injuring herself. Morningleaf lay down and waited. Just listening for what seemed like hours, until her eyes began to close.

Kaboom! Firemouth roared, waking Morningleaf, who didn't remember falling asleep. She scrambled to her hooves, her heart racing. The mountain shook, sounding like a thunderstorm. Loose rock and dust fell on Morningleaf, coating her in dirt. She swallowed the desire to bolt, forcing herself to hold still. Would the lava rush through the tubes? Would she be burned alive? Morningleaf's blood rushed through her limbs and muscles, urging her to run. She clamped her wings tight against her back; to panic in here was to die in here.

She stood still, waiting, listening, but no lava came to sweep her away—only a rush of beetles that had been disturbed by the shaking mountain. As their clattering bodies scurried past her, Morningleaf exhaled with relief. Bugs were preferable to lava.

She inched forward, creeping slowly so as not to alert Frostfire's team to her presence. After traveling a long distance, she settled into a steady gait and walked—for how long she did not know.

Days passed, and Morningleaf was still lost in the tubes. She counted the passing time by the hunger growing in her hollow belly. She'd known when the first day had passed because she'd gone without food that long before. The whistles of the sky-herder had come and gone as she searched the miles of tunnels. Clearly Larksong was communicating with the stallions, using her whistles to let them know where she was. They were helping one another, working as a team, so they wouldn't get lost in the maze. Morningleaf guessed they also took breaks to eat and drink. Periodically Firemouth roared, the tunnels shook, and more loose rocks tumbled onto her head.

Still, Morningleaf traveled, and listened.

She'd guessed another day had passed when her hungry belly had ceased being merely restless and took up a desperate, nagging clamor for food. Rats scurried busily through the tunnels, often skittering over her hooves and climbing up her tail. Morningleaf shoved them off her with her nose, curling her lip at their putrid scent and chiding herself for feeling envious of them. The rats were fat and unafraid. They were eating something, and she was not.

After another day or two, the painful pinch of hunger had been replaced by unbearable thirst—terrible and throat searing. Morningleaf's tongue swelled and her eyes dried out, feeling like shriveled grapes. Her heart slowed, weakening to a mouse-like beat. She lay down to rest, just for a minute, but once down, she feared she would not rise again.

Frostfire's mare had not given up her searching, but

Morningleaf realized she had to get out or she would die in the tubes. She made a plan and decided to travel only when she heard the mare whistling, like now, because only then could she be sure she was walking in the opposite direction.

Morningleaf staggered to her hooves, her legs shaking, threatening to buckle. Firemouth belched, and several creatures flew past her head—more bats, she guessed. Even after living here for days, her eyes had not adjusted to the total darkness. The tunnels were so black she couldn't see the whiskers on her muzzle. She walked slowly forward, feeling for new tunnels with her wings, all the while imagining Star's face when they'd said goodbye. She'd thought Nightwing was their greatest concern, but once again the greatest threat was coming from another herd.

She stumbled over loose rocks and swayed with spells of dizziness. Larksong's clicks and whistles bounced off the rock walls and gave Morningleaf a mental picture of the tunnels. *This is how bats see in the dark,* she thought. She also realized Frostfire's team would not give up their search. Frostfire was not the sort of captain who failed his missions. She hoped to lose them in the jungle, if she ever got out of the tubes.

Morningleaf walked for many more hours, twisting

and turning through the volcano, moving slower than a snail, still afraid of falling into a lava pit. She suddenly halted, pricking her ears. There it was again: air—a breeze! She followed it, creeping through another narrow tunnel. She tripped on a large rock, and her ankle twisted as her hoof slid off it. She bit back a squeal of pain and kept moving, limping now, her eyes too dry to make tears.

Seconds later Morningleaf heard the short call of a bird, followed by another, and she kept her ears trained on their singing. Soon the moist air of the jungle filtered into her nostrils. She turned a corner and gasped, overjoyed. There ahead of her was a sphere of light in an exit—a perfect circle in the rock and beyond it green trees and blue skies. She blinked rapidly, blinded by the sudden sunshine. She picked up each hoof slowly and carefully set it down, making no noise but moving faster. When she reached the end of the tube, she stopped, listening and smelling the wind before she dared stick out her head.

When she did, she saw she was on the northern side of Firemouth. The forest here was especially dense, and there was no sign of her captors. She stepped out and hobbled into the foliage. The leaves were wet from a recent rainfall. She lapped at them fiercely, taking the drops of water onto her tongue and swallowing, feeling the liquid drip down her dry throat and into her empty belly. The grasses below her hooves were also damp and fat with moisture. She ripped up hunks of foliage and chewed, not caring if she was eating weeds, but Morningleaf had learned from Sweetroot not to gorge herself after a long break from eating. After several minutes she forced herself to stop.

Already feeling much better, Morningleaf looked around her and stretched her wings. The trees were the tallest she'd ever seen. She knew Jungle Herd built sleeping nests in the heights, but their nesting grounds were not located near Firemouth. She walked deeper into the jungle, getting her bearings, her ears swiveling and her nostrils flaring. A lizard sprang off a low branch, hit the jungle floor, and scurried away, and the sudden movement spooked Morningleaf off the ground. She hovered a winglength above the path and decided to cruise through the forest this way since her injured ankle had begun to swell.

She was exhausted and weak, but needed to put distance between herself and Frostfire. So when she heard the voice behind her, she did not believe her ears.

"I've got you!"

She turned and gasped.

It was Frostfire.

31

JET STREAM

MORNINGLEAF CHOKED ON HER DESPAIR, FEELING all was lost. Frostfire pranced, waiting to see which way she would fly. His triumphant expression enraged her. Morningleaf whirled around. Maybe she could still escape. "You don't have me!" she whinnied, and then she darted straight up into the sky. Her body was weak, but anger fueled her muscles. All that mattered was escaping and warning Hazelwind and Echofrost about Rockwing's plans to invade Sun Herd's territory. She couldn't let Frostfire stop her.

The white captain zipped after her, snapping at her tail, but Morningleaf was smaller and could dodge quickly through the dense trees. She surged ahead, inspired by the legend of Raincloud, the bravest mare in the history of Anok. Morningleaf narrowed her eyes, flapping her wings harder, her heart pumping to the rhythm.

Behind her she heard Frostfire trumpeting for the others.

Morningleaf did not bother to look back. She kept her eyes trained on her path and took a deep breath, bolstering herself for the impossible thing she was about to do.

With her nose trained upward and her wings pushing her higher and higher, Morningleaf rose past the clouds and kept climbing. Behind her, she heard Frostfire's gasping breaths. Mountain Herd pegasi were too muscular and short winged for long, high flights. Morningleaf was small and long feathered, but she was quickly running out of oxygen as she surged higher.

Black spots sprinkled her vision, and her ears prickled from the devastating rays of the sun. Morningleaf dared a backward glance and saw Frostfire hovering far below, sapped, waiting for his sky herder, who was small and built to fly higher.

Morningleaf couldn't be in the sky when Larksong arrived. The mare would catch her in seconds. Morningleaf needed to ride a jet stream. It was the fastest way to fly, although the most dangerous. The jet stream wind currents ripped across the highest elevations at hurricane speeds. Only Desert Herd steeds were skilled at riding them. But it was Morningleaf's only chance to get away.

She flew higher, searching. *Where was the northern jet stream?* Morningleaf panicked, confused by the conflicting currents that battered her, until she finally encountered a wake. A wake meant a faster current was near, and this one was traveling north.

Frostfire guessed her plan and surged toward her, gulping for air. "Don't do it, Morningleaf. You won't survive!" He bared his teeth and lashed his tail as he flew closer, whipping apart the clouds.

Fury flooded her thoughts, and her heart slammed fresh blood through her veins. He didn't care about her; he just wanted to use her to control Star. She wouldn't let him capture her again. "Ancestors, be with me," Morningleaf nickered, and then she flew headfirst through the wake and into the northern jet stream.

Morningleaf shrieked as her body rocketed forward. Her ears smashed flat against her head, and her wings dragged behind her. She wasn't flying; she was blowing over the landscape like debris from a hurricane. Morningleaf ransacked her mind for information on jet streams. The old mare Mossberry had entertained the foals with tales of Spiderwing and Raincloud when Morningleaf was younger. Spiderwing was legendary for his fearlessness in all areas except one; he was terrified of jet streams. What had Mossberry said about them? The key to riding them was simple, but what was it? Morningleaf's heart thundered, distracting her.

Keep your nose straight.

Morningleaf heard Mossberry's voice as though the old mare were flying next to her.

Grip the current. Let the jet stream do the work.

Now Morningleaf remembered; jet streams weren't for flying, they were for riding. She needed to shape her wings around the current to keep her body straight, and she couldn't move her head until she was ready to exit.

Riding the streams can be managed by most pegasi, Mossberry had warned. *Exiting the streams is what kills them.*

A horrific chill rolled down Morningleaf's spine. If she died on exit, Star would blame Frostfire, and Star's anger concerned her. If the steeds of Anok thought he was tame, they were wrong. Star was just beginning to understand his power.

Morningleaf's body wavered as she tried to focus. She needed to pull her wings forward, to grip and hold the current, otherwise a simple cross breeze could knock her over and out of the jet stream. So far she'd been lucky not to encounter one. With her eyes half shut and blurry with wind tears, Morningleaf shrugged her small wings forward, feather by feather. A wrong move could result in the forceful winds snapping her bones or flipping her over, and then she would lose what little control she had.

It was terribly hard to keep her nose straight as she did this. From her peripheral vision she watched the landscape whiz by underneath her hooves. She was speeding across Anok, passing lakes, small mountains, and vast plains in the span of a breath. Her mouth and nose dried out, and every loose feather ripped free and twirled away as she followed the curve of the planet toward Sun Herd's territory.

Morningleaf strained hard against the walloping winds until her wings took the gentle shape of a curve and wrapped over the whistling jet stream, steadying her. It took all her strength to keep them in place, her jaw ached from clenching her teeth, and her muscles quivered on the verge of collapse.

Far ahead of her was Sun Herd's territory, but at the speed she was traveling, she would be there soon. Her heart pounded at the thought of exiting the jet stream, and she knew she was in terrible danger of not surviving. When she dipped her nose and dropped out of it, she would whip toward the ground faster than her wings could fly. If she could spread her wings and keep them from inverting, she had a chance at landing.

Morningleaf swallowed, her throat tight. She just wanted to arrive before Rockwing. If she could warn her brother, Hazelwind, as she fell, then it didn't matter if she landed or crashed after that. Morningleaf closed her eyes and made a wish. "Please may I not be too late."

32

REPLAY

STAR GLIDED TOWARD LAND, DESCENDING IN WIDE circles through the clouds when he reached Sun Herd's territory. It wasn't storming here, just raining. He shook the droplets out of his eyes and scanned for Hazelwind's herd.

He'd flown over Sky Meadow on his way—the one place he'd vowed never to return. The skeletons of the fallen Sun Herd pegasi were still visible. Sweet grasses had grown through the bones, and small creatures had built homes in them. Star knew the skeletons would soon disintegrate into the soil and nourish the roots. Someday new pegasi would graze on grasses grown from the marrow of the dead, and Star sighed with gentle understanding. Home wasn't just where you lived; it was where you died.

Star landed when he spotted the colorful feathers of Hazelwind and his followers. Hazelwind spotted him immediately and glided over, followed by Echofrost and the rest of his small herd. Shadepebble was with them, and she neighed a greeting when she saw Star. He neighed back and then spoke to Hazelwind. "I assume Shadepebble told you what's happened."

Hazelwind narrowed his eyes. "That Frostfire stole my sister, Rockwing plans to claim the Sun Herd lands, and Nightwing is returning to Anok?" asked Hazelwind. "Yes, Shadepebble informed me." He exhaled. "What I don't understand is why you're here, Star. You're not a warrior."

Hazelwind's words stung, and Star lowered his head. "I've come to help."

"Help us to our deaths, like you did in the north?" Hazelwind stamped his hoof. "You can guard the newborns." He turned his back on Star and returned to battle training his herd. Echofrost followed, refusing to look at him.

Star stood alone, feeling uprooted and lost. Hazelwind blamed him for all their bad luck and, he guessed, for Dawnfir's death. She had been Hazelwind's best friend next to Echofrost. And Echofrost had not forgiven Star either for Brackentail.

Shadepebble approached Star. "Don't worry," she nickered. "Frostfire won't hurt Morningleaf."

Star gazed into the eyes of the pink-feathered filly who'd been born a runt and a dud, and he saw only hope and kindness in her eyes. "Why are you helping us against your father? It's treason." Star was curious and astonished.

Shadepebble cut her gaze toward the weeping willow tree. "Follow me, and I'll show you."

Star followed her to the tree. Lying in the grass beneath its long, sad branches was the figure of a white pegasus stallion. They approached him and halted. "This is Clawfire," said Shadepebble, her voice hitching with pride and sorrow.

"Isn't he the captain who kidnapped you?" asked Star.

Shadepebble knelt beside the stallion, smoothing his wet brow with her wing. "Yes. He saved me from an ice tiger, but it bit him here and here." She pointed to two gaping flesh wounds that were covered in flies. "Hazelwind found him as he was leaving the Ice Lands, and they carried him here."

Star watched the semiconscious stallion shiver in the cool shade. His hide was stained with sweat, an old, jagged scar marked his face, and he was big and heavily muscled, like most Snow Herd stallions. Star could only imagine the terror Shadepebble must have felt when he'd yanked her out of the sky and stolen her from her home. "I don't understand why you care for him," Star admitted.

"I know," said Shadepebble. "Someday I'll tell our story, but now is not the time." Clawfire moaned with pain. A large tear formed and rolled down Shadepebble's cheek. "I'm not committing treason, Star." She looked up at the sky. "When Clawfire and I were in the Ice Lands, he showed me the lights of the Ancestors. You know how they live together in peace in the golden meadow?"

Star grunted, thinking of Morningleaf and how much the two fillies were alike. "I've heard that," he said.

"Well, if they can do it there, I think we can live like that here. I know we can." Her eyes were bright and optimistic. "My sire taught me I couldn't trust foreign steeds, but he was wrong. Clawfire earned my trust." Shadepebble sighed. "Someday the herds will unite."

Star's heart ached for those words to be true. "You think so?" he asked.

She wiped the tears off her face. "Yes. I believe it's possible, and I think you can help us." She looked again at the sky, which was cloudy and blue. Star saw the hope glowing in her dark eyes, and he realized she believed in him like Morningleaf did, with her whole heart.

"Move over," he said quietly. "I'll heal this stallion for you."

Shadepebble leaped out of his way and pranced nearby, unable to contain her excitement. "Thank you," she whispered.

Star gathered the golden fire in his belly, warm and comforting, and he let it curl up from his gut and crawl through his neck until he felt the hot vibrations in the back of his throat. He opened his mouth and bathed the white stallion in yellow spears of light. The stallion floated off the grass, just a featherlength, and he moaned as though waking up from a long sleep. When his hide was shiny, his wounds healed, and his breathing normal, Star closed his mouth and the crackling hiss of his power retreated.

Clawfire stood, and Shadepebble raced to his side. They nuzzled, exchanging breath, and then the stallion faced Star and bowed his head. "Starwing," he neighed, low and rumbling, "you have my gratitude forever."

Star ignored the title Starwing and just nodded. He looked at Shadepebble. He didn't have much time to talk sense into her if Rockwing was on his way. "I know you're planning to trade yourself to stop your sire from taking this territory and for the safe return of Morningleaf. Please don't."

Clawfire jerked his head toward Shadepebble, and she set her jaw, reminding Star again of Morningleaf.

"You two should fly away. Now, before Rockwing arrives," urged Star.

"No!" whinnied Shadepebble, slicing the air with her black tail. "I made a promise. I have to help Morningleaf. She's my friend. And maybe I can explain to my sire that he's been wrong about the other herds. I have to go back. I have to try."

Clawfire snapped his eyes to Star. "Is Morningleaf the blue-winged chestnut you saved on your birthday?"

Star clenched his jaw. "Yes. But I'll get Morningleaf back another way."

"There is no other way," said Shadepebble. "I have to do this, for all of us, to stop the coming bloodshed." Her expression was anguished.

"Please," begged Star. "I'll stop Rockwing, and I'll find Morningleaf myself." He knew Morningleaf, and she would never forgive him if he didn't prevent this.

"No," neighed Shadepebble. "You can't fight my sire; he'll kill Morningleaf if you do, and then you'll never get her back." Shadepebble's eyes widened as something caught her eye behind Star's back. "It's too late!" she whinnied. "My sire is here."

She lifted off and flew toward Hazelwind just as Rockwing's battle cry rang across the open plain. Star's gut twisted. Rockwing had brought his army. Over a thousand warriors were charging toward them, facing Hazelwind, who had no real army.

Forgetting his wings, Star galloped like a horse toward Hazelwind's front line, jumping over the brush and deep ditches. Hazelwind and his army of mares, yearlings, stallions, and elderly lifted off the ground, facing Rockwing's approaching army. At the very front of Hazelwind's line hovered Echofrost, her sleek body poised for battle.

Star's heart shattered. His friends would not survive this war—this massacre. It was like time had unwound, and Star's friends had to replay their final battle once again in a cruel twist of fate. The power in Star's belly pranced on the thin divide between healing and destroying, awaiting Star's command.

Star shuddered, terrified, not of Rockwing but of himself. He would not let Hazelwind lose this battle. If that meant Star had to become a killer, a destroyer of pegasi, then he would cross that line, and then he would leave Anok and never return.

33

A FILLY FOR A FILLY

FIVE WARRIORS PEELED OFF HAZELWIND'S MINUS-cule front line and snatched Shadepebble, who was flying toward them as fast as she could. Star's pulse flowed with her; his blood filled his ears like a raging river.

Star overheard Shadepebble speaking to Hazelwind's stallions. "Remember, I'm your captive. You have to make it look real."

The stallions blinked at her but understood her meaning; they would have to hurt her. One grabbed her pink feathers in his mouth and bit down so hard she squealed in pain.

Star staggered, feeling ill. This was getting out of control.

The warrior stallions escorted Shadepebble to Hazel-wind, and then Hazelwind took her to his front line and ordered his stallions to hold her still. She definitely looked like a captive to the Mountain Herd army.

In the distance, Rockwing recognized his filly. Shade-pebble's pink feathers and her heavily speckled hide were hard to miss. He held up a wing. "Ho," Rockwing neighed, and his army landed. Rockwing's jaw gaped at the sight of Shadepebble under the control of Hazelwind. He marched his army closer, and then they stopped and Rockwing con-tinued forward with his captains until Hazelwind could hear him. "Let her go."

"You have Morningleaf," said Hazelwind. "I will trade your filly for my sister. And then you will go back to your home."

Rockwing snorted. "I don't have your filly."

Hazelwind lashed his tail. "Your captain Frostfire took her. Return her to us."

Rockwing pinned his ears and ordered his front line forward.

Hazelwind nodded to his stallions, and Shadepebble was slammed to the grass. The impact knocked the air from her lungs, and Star lurched toward her but stopped when she glared at him and shook her head. Two of

Hazelwind's stallions knelt on her wings, ready to break them. Shadepebble sucked at the wind, desperate for air. Star had to remind himself that this was an act.

"Do not advance," warned Hazelwind.

Rockwing refused to look at Shadepebble, and he gave the order for his line to continue their advance.

"Papa!" Shadepebble whinnied. "Help me."

Now Rockwing looked at her, but his army kept coming.

Hazelwind nodded at a stallion and he bent her wing harder, making her squeal again. Star pranced frantically, forcing himself not to come to her aid.

But the ruse worked. Rockwing stopped his advancing stallions.

"Bring me Morningleaf or I will break her flight bones," threatened Hazelwind, bluffing.

Rockwing narrowed his eyes. "I am taking this land today," he said. "And I will bring my filly home to her dam . . . dead or alive." Rockwing ordered his first battalion of five hundred warriors forward, and he sent two more around to flank each side of Hazelwind's gangly army.

Star exhaled, realizing Rockwing was desperate. The Mountain Herd warriors' ribs were showing, and their eyes were dull. Rockwing's herd was starving to death, and Shadepebble would die anyway if her sire didn't make this move to take Sun Herd's lands.

Star exchanged glances with Hazelwind. They nodded as understanding flashed between them. Trading Shadepebble would not stop this war.

"Charge!" whinnied Star. He and Hazelwind lifted off. Star set his eyes on Rockwing.

Fifteen hundred Mountain Herd soldiers surrounded Hazelwind and Star with teeth bared. Shadepebble trembled. "What now?" she cried out to Star.

Just then a sharp whinny rang from the clouds.

Everyone looked up, and Star's heart skidded to a halt. A blue-winged filly was crashing toward land in a spiraling nosedive.

"Morningleaf!" Star bolted from the field and darted into the sky.

She was spinning and twisting, and her wings appeared broken and useless. She plummeted at a speed Star had never before witnessed.

Echofrost kicked off and soared behind him. "She's fallen out of a jet stream!"

Star's heart restarted, pounding against his chest and threatening to explode. Only Desert Herd pegasi knew the secret to exiting jet streams. Tears welled in his eyes as he realized Morningleaf had escaped Frostfire and rushed here to save Hazelwind, her brother, but she was too late, and in a few seconds she would be dead.

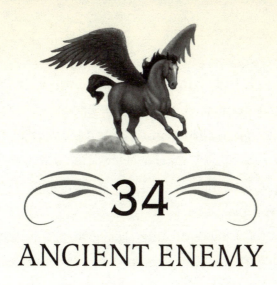

34

ANCIENT ENEMY

STAR FLEW TOWARD MORNINGLEAF, PANIC throttling his breath. He couldn't catch her at the speed she was falling. She was a blur of aqua and chestnut, and her white socks stabbed the clouds as she tumbled upside down.

Star soared below her, devising how to save her, but she was dropping so fast. If he tried to catch her, both their bodies would break on impact. He spread his wings, hovering like a newborn with his back legs dangling and his neck arching toward her. There was one thing he could try. He exhaled starfire in a wide beam, guiding it toward her. Her body crashed into the supernatural light, and it slowed her, but she was still falling, too fast.

He angled his wings, letting his own body fall backward, and he pushed the starfire harder—outward and upward—concentrating on floating her, but she was falling through it. He glanced below and saw the meadow rushing toward them both. The watching pegasi scattered out of the impact zone.

Star took a breath, and the golden light flickered. Morningleaf rolled over, and he saw her round, wild eyes. He dug into his power and pushed up everything he had, and the starfire burst forth, glittering and golden, washing out every other color and blinding the pegasi in the meadow.

Morningleaf splayed her legs, finally floating. Star had caught her in his beam of fire. He guided her down gently until her hooves touched the grass one at a time and she was standing before him, all of her injuries healed. Star closed his mouth and extinguished the light. Morningleaf shook her head, dazed, and everyone stared at her.

Rockwing and Hazelwind stood at the front of their armies, facing each other, as if time had stopped. Then a flash of crimson caught Star's attention, and he saw that Thundersky, Silverlake, and Bumblewind had finally arrived. They joined Echofrost and galloped to Morningleaf's side as Thundersky landed next to his son,

Hazelwind. Star and Morningleaf were both shaking. "I'm too late," she whispered.

Rockwing scanned the sky from which Morningleaf fell and brayed at her. "Where is Frostfire?"

"I escaped him," Morningleaf answered, wheezing. "He's still at the lava tubes, in Jungle Herd's territory. The tunnels have re-formed since the collapse hundreds of years ago. He thought he could hide me inside, but I used them to get away."

"He hid you beneath Firemouth? The volcano?"

Morningleaf set her jaw. "He tried."

Rockwing arched his neck and bellowed at his army. "You hear that? This filly escaped Frostfire! And he failed to return Shadepebble to me. Frostfire is banished from Mountain Herd." His eyes swept the faces of his soldiers. "If he returns, kill him on sight."

Star pinned his ears, looking from Morningleaf to Hazelwind, to Bumblewind and Echofrost, and then back to Rockwing and his warriors. They were all prepared to die for Sun Herd's land.

Star flared his wings, snapping golden sparks across the grass, and every pegasi halted, staring at him. Star met their eyes. He saw fear, hatred, and violence churning inside his friends and his enemies alike. He glanced at

Morningleaf. Her mouth was open, and she shrank from him. He saw she was afraid of what he might do. Star turned away from her and stood in the center of the two armies, hunting for the words that might stop the battle.

But before Star could utter a sound, a sharp, crackling whinny swooped across the field, causing the pegasi to crane their necks and prick their ears. Star lifted his wings and his eyes toward the sky, squinting into the hazy clouds. A giant black shadow swept across the meadow, blocking out the sun. All eyes turned up, and Star, for a second, thought he was having one of his visions.

A black pegasus glided over their heads. He was gaunt and hollow faced and flew on wings too large for his body, like a bat. Star gasped. He wasn't dreaming. This was no vision. This was Nightwing.

The pegasi, even the warriors, flinched in terror, and some stampeded into the woods. The newborns darted under their mothers' bellies, bleating, feeling the panic but not understanding it. Star watched the fierce steeds, who normally raced into battle, crumble around him. As he witnessed their incredible fear of Nightwing, he finally understood why so many had wanted to execute Star when he was still a harmless foal. Star could have turned into this—and some believed he still might.

Nightwing nickered, but it sounded like the distant rumble of thunder, menacing. He landed in the center of the field and faced Star. "There you are," he said in a voice that crinkled like aged leaves.

Star reeled. The Destroyer's breath smelled like rotting flesh and dead trees. Star shook his head, still not believing this was real. Morningleaf charged across the grass and skidded into him, out of breath. She turned and faced Nightwing. Star tensed, wishing she would fly to safety. "Why are you here?" Star whinnied to Nightwing. "What do you want?"

Nightwing clacked his yellowed teeth at Morningleaf and tossed his dry, haggard mane, but his eyes glowed bright, the color of twin silver moons. "When you received your starfire, you woke me, black foal. *You* brought me here." He reared and slammed his hooves against the soil, his power flooding it. Sparks popped across the wet grass, setting it on fire.

Morningleaf and Star flinched, and screams erupted around them as more steeds raced for the woods or galloped into the sky. Others stood frozen, their eyes bulging. Bumblewind and Echofrost, inched closer to Star, their heads low, ears pinned at Nightwing.

Nightwing pranced around Star, flicking his tail.

Star circled, keeping his eyes trained on him. The ancient stallion was bone thin, and his dull hair was brittle and sparse, like grass in the fall. Star was heavier and round with muscle, but Nightwing was older, and his coarse hide sparkled with silver fire.

Rockwing glided toward them, avoiding the patches of hot flames, and he touched down next to Nightwing, his eyes mad with excitement. "Sir?" he said with a bow of his head. "I have a proposal."

Star gaped, stunned. The over-stallion of Mountain Herd could only want one thing from Nightwing: a pact. The Destroyer blinked at Rockwing, also seeming stunned. Star used the moment to push Morningleaf gently with his wing. "Go, please," he whispered, urging her away, his eyes pleading. For once she listened to him without hesitation, edging toward her mother, and Star was grateful.

Rockwing folded his wings, waiting for permission to continue.

Nightwing opened his mouth as if to respond, but instead he roared silver fire at Rockwing, and the magnificent spotted stallion burst into flames. Star reared away from the inferno, and Rockwing's screech of pain echoed all the way to the Blue Mountains. His feathers evaporated, then his flesh, and then his bones, until he was reduced to a pile of gray ash. Nightwing clapped his wings over the soot, and Rockwing's remains swirled away with the wind.

"Father!" screamed Shadepebble. Clawfire snatched her and held her back as her tears dropped fast and furious.

Anok was spinning around Star, falling apart and re-forming. Rockwing was dead, the Destroyer was awake, and Star stood in the center of it like an observer—like a dud. He had to do something!

"You want *me*, not them!" Star neighed, coughing on the smoke from the fires. He pawed the grass. "Well, come and get me." With a quick glance at his friends, Star reared, coiling back his hooves. Nightwing also reared.

"No, Star," whinnied Morningleaf. "Don't fight him!"

Star blinked, and time slowed. He shut her out and focused his thoughts on destruction. If it was true he'd woken Nightwing, then it was time to put the ancient stallion back to sleep.

The few steeds remaining crouched, ducking as though they could hide from what was coming next. Even the birds stopped flying as a hush fell over the pegasi—their battle forgotten—for each of them understood that the Destroyer had returned to Anok.

ACKNOWLEDGMENTS

I'D LIKE TO THANK THE ADULTS AND CHILDREN who've shared their love of the Guardian Herd series with me. It's exciting to hear about your favorite characters, answer your questions about the series, and share my writing tips with you. I've also enjoyed all the amazing pegasi art, which is featured on my website. Seeing my characters from your eyes and meeting the new characters you create is fun and inspiring.

Thank you for dreaming with me!

For more information on the series or to contact Jennifer, please visit her website (www.jenniferlynnalvarez.com).

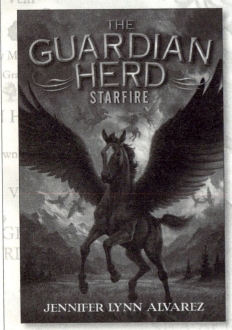
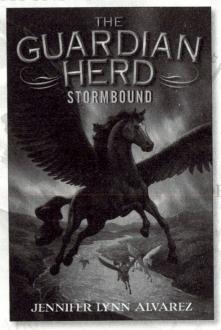